FIND ESCHER

FINDING ESCHER

ROXANNE DINSDALE

First Published in 2024 by Roxanne Dinsdale

Copyright © 2024 Roxanne Dinsdale

The right of Roxanne Dinsdale to be identified as the author of this Work has been asserted by them in accordance with sections 77 and 78 of the Copyright, Designs and Patents Act 1988

All rights reserved. No part of this publication may be reproduced, stored in a retrieval system, copied in any form or by any means, electronic, mechanical, photocopying, recording or otherwise transmitted without written permission from the author.

Copy Editing and Typesetting by Laura B Empowered Words
www.laurab-empoweredwords.com

Cover Design by Steph Buncher
www.stephbuncherdesign.co.uk

I'd like to dedicate this book to those I've ignored, even when they offered tea. Thanks for not deserting me.

And to Mark, just one word... 'Ditto.'

Thank you to English poet Ann Taylor who's work was the inspiration behind Escher's poem.

Lastly, special thanks to Laura from Laura B Empowered Words and Steph from Steph Buncher Design for their help and knowledge in producing what I hope you will agree is a page turning book with twists around every corner.

PROLOGUE

The boy lay beneath the filth-streaked blanket. The smell of urine unnoticed by its familiarity. His only possessions were the sounds in his head, sounds which could roar or be as delicate and quiet as he wished. Precious words of paradise, caged in his head for safety's sake. He knew from experience that if he were to release them to the air, say them out loud, they would return to him with pain. A slap, a pinch, sometimes worse.

The story of his young life was written in violence and abuse. The slap of a hand, a full stop; a kick, an exclamation; an hour's abuse, a sentence. This was his narrative, days equalled paragraphs. Months were chapters and the coming of each new year saw the end of another book of horror. He memorised these tomes and, as terrifying as they were, he did not and would not let himself forget. He knew one day he'd burn those books in the library of his mind along with the person who'd enabled the writing of every pain-filled and degrading syllable.

ONE

It was mid-July and much hotter in Sicily than weather reports had predicted. The sun blazed down on Lucy, inconsiderate to her current predicament, taunting her with its joviality, as if it knew she was unable to revel in her surroundings and show how much she enjoyed being in a place as beautiful as Savoca. Lucy's visit was a sombre one, she was arranging the funeral of her last remaining relative.

Her great aunt, and namesake, Sofia Lucia Randazzo had managed to evade the grim reaper until she was just short of one hundred and six years old. When death finally caught her, it was in the middle of the night as she slept a calm and dreamless sleep, the clock continued to tick, the cat purred, but not a sound came from the old lady.

Night lifted and the light of day brought with it the delivery boy. As was usual on a Monday he carried with him a warm, freshly baked loaf of bread wrapped in paper.

Sofia had loved the first cut of her weekly bread, the smell of the sesame seeds, the crunch of the crust. Each day for her lunch, she'd slice two thin pieces, drizzle them with olive oil and add some finely diced tomato. Toward the end of the week, as the bread became stale, she'd eat it with a little pecorino and some anchovies. In winter, the bread would be plated and placed by the open fire to warm, but in summer she'd leave it on the kitchen windowsill under a muslin cloth, where the heat of the sun would intensify the flavours. When the aroma hit the air, Sofia knew it was time to eat and she'd take her tasty meal to her seat in the garden and balance the plate on her skilful knees as she ate. If it rained, she'd stay inside at the kitchen table and listen to the music of the drops and splashes as they fell on the tiled roof.

The delivery boy pulled the bell cord, no answer, he walked to the rear of the villa and knocked loudly on the door as he knew she didn't hear well. He waited patiently imagining the old lady rising from her chair, shuffling the twelve or so feet across the room and opening the door. He stared at the handle expecting it to move, but it didn't, he waited for several seconds before putting an ear to the wood, no sound came from inside. Cautiously he entered, calling Sofia's name. Still no reply. He laid the bread down on the chopping board, and knowing in his heart what had happened, he left the villa and ran to the church to alert the priest.

There was a lot for Lucy to do in Sicily, although none of it much fun. The funeral had to be arranged, translators, lawyers and estate agents had to be sought out, instructed, and paid, and as well as all that Lucy had to organise a wake for friends and neighbours too.

The day of the funeral Lucy woke earlier than she would have liked, despite re-positioning pillows and sheets on her great aunts soft and ancient bed, nothing would bring back the sleep she hankered after. Reluctantly she washed and dressed, then deciding it would be an idea to walk to the church and pay her last respects privately, she left the villa and set off through the village streets.

At the church, the heavily carved wooden doors were already open. Lucy peered inside, the place lay empty and silent, not even the whistle of a distant caretaker was to be heard. She thought about shouting hello, to let it be known she was there, but the air was still, the silence poised, making it totally inappropriate to utter anything above a whisper. The casket lay open ahead.

Walking between the pews Lucy watched her great aunt's face reveal itself at each forward step. First a tuft of grey hair, followed by forehead, eyelids, the bridge of her nose, her prominent cheek bones highlighted with doll pink blush, lips an incongruous red and finally her chin, once proud and strong, with age had become hardly distinguishable from her neck. What once was full of life, now lay frail and vacant as a sundried snail shell. The old lady's flaccid arms were folded across her chest, their skin corrugated like a multitude of thick rubber bands lain one alongside the other. A sudden compulsion to jab a finger into the soft tanned flesh came over Lucy, she glanced around the church and up at the fat stone faces of several cherubs and decided against it.

Looking back at her great aunt, she wondered why on earth someone would want to apply such garish makeup to the cheeks of a dead old maid and with a paintbrush by the look of it.

Dead, the word resonated in Lucy's head and the realisation she was alone with a corpse hit her, a shudder jittered down her spine, at the same time a feeling of cloying tendrils made its way from her legs toward her torso. Panicked, she turned and bolted down the aisle toward the door, shaking herself intermittently to escape the invisible hands which attempted to wring out her heart and lungs.

Once outside the awful feeling lifted, Lucy took control of her ragged breath, by pursing her lips and blowing out slowly. As she sipped air back into her lungs the sweet calming fragrance of Sulla rising from the valley below came with it. She watched the deep red flowers swirl uncontrollably, puppeted by the force created as cool sea breeze hit hot island air. The sun obligingly bloomed from behind a flimsy cloud and Lucy felt encouraged to seat herself on the low stone wall to the front of the building. She gazed out to the horizon and watched the boats as they navigated the sea and wondered where they had come from, what they were carrying and where they were headed.

A vision of a very old and tattered photograph given to her by her great aunt back in America, when Lucy was just six years old, popped into her head. The picture was of her great aunt when she was young, maybe in her late twenties, she was in profile on an obviously windy day as her hair was almost horizontal. Her great aunt said it was to remind Lucy she wasn't alone in the world. She placed it in Lucy's hand on the day Lucy's mother was buried. After the funeral service her great aunt returned to Sicily, leaving Lucy in the hands of foster carers. It was the first and last time they ever met.

Lucy realised why she'd thought of the picture at that moment, it was because she was sitting in the exact same spot her great aunt sat in the photo. Lucy, curious about what her great aunt could have been looking at, turned her head in the same direction and found herself staring across the hill toward the museum which lay on the far side of Savoca.

Two

Lucy closed the lid on the last box containing her great aunt's clothes and placed it on top of several others filled with ornaments and usable kitchen ware, ready to be delivered to a thrift shop in the village. The furniture remained in situ for the time being, awaiting the valuer, as did several pieces of jewellery and two paintings depicting quaint scenes of peasant families. There was one particular item, to which Lucy was drawn. A mirror. A rectangle of glass surrounded by a filigree metallic frame. She walked over to where it stood on a small table by her aunt's bed, picked it up and was surprised at how heavy it was for its size. There was some crumpled brown paper around its neck tied on with string, Lucy flipped the mirror over. Inside the back of the frame was a bronze disc, a flat handle was attached to it which extended into the neck and the stand of the mirror. There were no makers marks, but it was old, Lucy could tell that much.

As she placed it back on the table the paper from its neck fell to the floor, unfurling slightly revealing its original envelope shape. Lucy picked it up, the letters S.L.R, Lucy's initials, were written on the front, she slid her little finger into the gap of the fold and used it like a letter opener. Inside was a single sheet of paper, bearing a sentence in Italian which began with the word Sophia. Lucy was immediately excited and wondered if her great aunt had left the mirror specifically for her. Thank goodness she'd not boxed it up with the rest of the junk. She folded the note, popped it in her jeans pocket, took the mirror, wrapped it in a shawl from the top box and placed it in her suitcase, just as she heard her taxi pull up outside. It felt strange to be leaving so soon, she would have gladly stayed in such a beautiful place for another week or two, maybe forever. But work beckoned and money was short, maybe one day she'd return.

An hour or so later Lucy exited the taxi and took a short stroll through Catania airport to where she would catch her plane. As she walked she took out her passport and the letter came with it, she kept it in her hand until she boarded her flight, eager to find a translator.

Her seat in the aisle was next to a woman wearing a Tee printed with the words Texas Forever and reading a copy of Ladies' Day magazine. Lucy noted the woman's left arm was extremely sunburned and wondered what had happened for her to get only a single limb to that state of raging red. She took her seat, buckled up and attempted to look out of the window, but her efforts were thwarted by the woman and her magazine. The plane started its take off. The woman unconcerned with the fidgeting meerkat next to her, turned to the cookery page, rested the bottom edge of the magazine on her barrel of a stomach and began perusing a recipe for Braciole. Lucy, fearing she'd miss what could be her last ever sight of Sicily, swiped the magazine from the woman's fingers and placed it in the rack along with the flight information.

'Just until we get away from the island.' Lucy said, adding a disarming smile to soften the impact of her actions.

The woman scowled in annoyance. 'Rude.'

'Look what you're missing.' Lucy gestured toward the window.

The woman looked out, unimpressed with the passing jigsaw of brownish green farmland. Lucy on the other hand saw the beauty of endless fields, the farmhouses with their many outbuildings, the lines of trees along slim roads and the quaint towns of buff-coloured houses. The woman said nothing, took back her magazine, flicked through to the Braciole recipe and settled back to reading. This time Lucy didn't protest, she'd remembered the paper, and her thoughts turned to what was written on it. She peered down the aisle, most of the passengers looked like tourists and the thought of having to ask multiple people if they could translate for her and then having to explain about her great aunt, the mirror and her trip, wasn't something Lucy relished. God forbid if they then wanted to impart the banalities of their holiday to her. Lucy balked at the idea and instead called over the stewardess and explained her predicament. Within minutes the stewardess returned with another member of the cabin crew and the script was translated.

Sophia, see me here as I see you in my heart. Always S.

Before Lucy could explain the letter was not from some vacation romance, the crew member was called away to calm a fearful flyer.

Lucy stared at the scrawl, convinced it confirmed the mirror was meant for her, the message made sense, she would indeed see her great aunt when she looked in the mirror, as they were incredibly similar in appearance at the same age. Another thing crossed Lucy's mind, so far, this heavy piece of bling was the only thing she had to show for all she'd done in Sicily. The money she was to inherit from the sale of the villa and its contents would be tied up with lawyers back in Italy for some time. She hoped eventually it would reimburse her for the cost of her trip, the funeral and wake, and maybe even leave her enough for a bigger apartment.

***

In the thin grey light of the New York morning Lucy's skin looked pale and delicate, hard to imagine only eight days before she'd been in sunny Sicily. She adjusted the angle of her great aunt's mirror and contemplated a newly acquired fine line under her right eye.

Getting old.

For some reason her mind turned to Tom her ex, and briefly she wondered where he was and what he was doing. Taking some tweezers from a small container on the shelf she plucked away at the few black dots of eyebrow hairs that had grown insidiously from her skin overnight. A layer of condensation fanned over the mirror, and as she tried to wipe it away she saw a reflection of Tom, naked from the waist up, a baby held to his chest. Instinctively she turned, but there was no Tom, just her robe hanging from the hook on the bathroom door. She rubbed her forehead, squeezed her eyes shut for a second and surmised the vision was nothing more than sleep deprivation.

Returning to the mirror, she wiped a fresh layer of condensation away and continued to pluck her eyebrows.

When they'd met, Tom had been a gym addict, the type who trained for self-improvement and health rather than to impress others. Initially he'd tolerated Lucy's cool independence. He gave her space, emotional and actual, but as the months went by, he became tired of waiting for her to show feelings for him, feelings that were more than sexual. But the closer he tried to get to Lucy the more distant she became. She stayed later at work and spent more time with her friends. Finally, Tom was forced to find an antidote to Lucy's unyielding nature, and its name was Andrea.

He'd cried when he told Lucy he couldn't continue their relationship as it was too one-way and that he'd found someone else. Lucy acted upset, although she was careful not to go overboard as she didn't want Tom to renege on his leaving her, but she laid it on enough not to seem like a cold-hearted bitch, she even managed to squeeze out a few crocodile tears, of which she was immensely proud.

As Tom gave her one last guilt-ridden hug, Lucy made a mental note to include a little salty eyed sadness in future break ups, it was a nice touch.

Months later she heard on the girlfriend grapevine about Tom and Andrea's marriage and the imminent arrival of baby Lamar. She'd been happy for him, genuinely happy.

Lucy wasn't interested in all this forever business, her relationships were about immediacy, about sex and above all else, her being in control. Her modus operandi was to reel a guy in, have fun, make him want her and when she'd used him up, she'd discard him without pity or shame. Because she could. Because it was her life, and she made the rules.

Lucy placed some shadow concealer on the underside of her eyes and with the tip of her middle finger patted it outside corner to inner and back again, like she'd seen girls do on the YouTube tutorials.

Her phone alarm went off, a reminder she'd only got ten minutes left to get out of the apartment or risk being late for work.

Three

In her tiny windowless office at Maniac Locations, Lucy scoured the Internet. A new client needed buildings in which to film part of a zombie movie and their specific requirements didn't fit anything already on the company's database. The job took a lot longer than Lucy anticipated and her morning slipped away in a frustration of heart leaps followed by sighs. The pressure was on to come up with something by end of day, Maniac Locations had a reputation for acquiring some of the most prestigious and unusual film spaces in New York's seven boroughs. That reputation was built on the knowledge, tenacity, and bullshitting ability, of one employee, Lucy Randazzo.

'Hey…Hey, don't make me ask you again girl, you want coffee or not?' Lucy's friend and colleague, Chinah, screwed up the sheet of paper in her hand and threw it at Lucy's head through the gap she'd made in the doorway.

Lucy smoothed her hair and continued to move her mouse over a worn Super Girl mat.

'I'm busy Chinah, buzz off, I'm still…hang on what's this…' she held up her hand palm toward Chinah, her eyes still on the computer screen. 'Got it.' She said triumphantly.

'Girl, you gotta stop sometime, take a break.' Chinah stepped into the room and folded her arms across her huge bosoms, causing a multi directional escape of flesh.

'I got a spare bagel.' She trilled.

'Busy.' Lucy replied, her gaze still on the monitor.

Chinah's chubby hand whizzed in front of Lucy's face and snatched the mouse from her fingers.

'Stop messing about, seriously, I'm busy.' Lucy swiped at the mouse and grabbed nothing but air.

'Eat the bagel, get the mouse'. Chinah said, disappearing into the hallway.

Lucy took one last glance at her computer screen, then reluctantly followed her colleague to the staff room.

Two hot buttered bagels, two mugs of coffee and a copy of the New York Wire, lay on a small table, made level by the addition of folded gum wrappers beneath one of its legs. Chinah took a coffee and one of the bagels, hooked her foot around the leg of a chair, dragged it with her to the doorway and sat down.

'You really don't trust me, do you?' Lucy laughed.

'Eat the bagel, get the mouse.' Chinah nodded down to her chest. Lucy followed her gaze and saw the mouse poking out from amongst an abundance of cleavage. 'Ok you win.' She smirked picking up the remaining bagel.

'You at least gonna sit?' Chinah pointed to a chair next to Lucy. 'I tell you, you gonna get sick like my aunt Mae if you don't eat.'

'Oh Jesus, please not the aunt Mae speech again.' Lucy reluctantly sat.

The New York Wire caught her eye, a quarter page picture of a smiling young boy was on the cover. She twisted the newspaper round to face her, the bold font read…

Amber alert issued, for missing 6-year-old.
Police are becoming increasingly concerned for missing six-year-old boy, Bodie Rodgers…

'Still not found the little guy.' Chinah said solemnly. 'He's dead for sure.'

'Chinah!' Lucy spat bagel across the floor.

'They think someone's grabbed him up, that's why the Amber alert. He'll be in the Hud' or Harlem, feedn' the fish.' Chinah added.

'Oh, you're just sick.' Lucy shoved her chair back, stood up, stuck the remainder of the bagel in her mouth, grabbed her coffee and nodded for Chinah to move.

'He's someone's kid.' Lucy mumbled; bagel held precariously between her teeth. She dipped forward with speed and precision, whisked the mouse out from between Chinahs' bosoms and popped it in the pocket of her cargo pants.

'Outta my personal space.' Chinah blustered and clasped her hand to her chest.

Lucy took the bagel from her mouth.

'Babe, with the size of them ta-tas, everyone and everything's in your personal space'.

FOUR

On her way home Lucy took a detour, she'd read of the imminent demolition of several buildings and was hopeful one of them could be used for the zombie movie. No luck, the first was too far gone, probably empty for years, it had been pretty much destroyed by vandals and arsonists. The other had been a car lot, consisting of a centrally placed single storey glass fronted building, not the sort of ramshackle atmospheric place Lucy was looking for.

It was already getting dark by the time Lucy turned the key in her apartment door, she needed to get to work early the next day to start on the backlog of jobs the zombie movie had caused, so after eating a cream cheese bagel, a banana, and a yoghurt several days out of date, she decided to hit the mattress.

She made her way to the bathroom, picked up

a cleanser pad and began to remove her eyeliner, careful to negotiate her way around her eyes without disturbing her mascara, if she slept on her back, it would stay on without smudging, which would give her an extra few minutes in the morning. Black eye makeup was all Lucy wore during the day, unless she were on a date or out with the girls, then she'd add a little rose-coloured lipstick.

She was fortunate enough to have blemish free olive skin, bright hazel eyes, a charming smile, and hair a glossy shade of chocolate. Lucy had what you'd call 'Goldilocks' looks, not too beautiful to be intimidating and not plain enough to go unnoticed. The addition of an amazing figure meant men were drawn to her regardless of what she deemed to be flaws, her nose slightly too wide to suit her face and the single dimple in her right cheek, a feature she associated with little girls or cute dolls, she thought of it as a separate entity, something which endeavoured to undermine her strength as a woman.

The TV was on in the lounge, the theme for the local news played out and was followed by the anchor reporting that six-year-old Bodie Rodgers was still missing…

What's happened to you kid?

She took a Q-Tip from the jar on the windowsill, dipped it in eye make-up remover and returned her gaze to the mirror. What was reflected made her recoil in shock, she stumbled back several steps and fumbled behind her for the doorknob, not daring to take her eyes off the vision in the glass. Opening the door, she shuffled round it, backed out and slammed it shut. Disbelief circled her brain as she hugged herself protectively.

What was that? It couldn't have been real, maybe I'm tired, maybe I've drunk too much coffee.

She stepped back and steadied herself against the wall, it felt safe and solid, she wanted to stay there and stare at the bathroom door until someone came to reassure her, but she knew that wasn't going to happen.

Come on get a grip, open the door, it's obviously something stupid.

'It's just something stupid,' she repeated out loud. But even so, to be safe she didn't want to open the door face on, so she moved to the wall on the side of the door, placed her hand on the cool doorknob, turned it as far round as she could and pushed ever so slightly until the door was open just a slither.

Fuuuuuuuck! Don't let me see anything, don't let me see anything, don't let me see anything.

She narrowed her eyes, clamped her hands on either side of her neck, inadvertently forming a measly protective shield for her body with her forearms. She nudged the door with her foot, it opened a little further, but not enough to see inside. She tried again, this time with a kick, more forceful than she'd intended. The door flung back, the handle hit the bathroom wall tiles, ricocheted off and juddered noisily to a stop. Nothing seemed amiss. She straightened up, stepped tentatively into the room and looked at the mirror. Relief coursed through her as she saw it reflected nothing but the ceiling light and the top of the door behind her. She stepped forward to take a closer look and noticed the Q-Tip's she'd been using were in the basin soaking up runnels of scummy water. She gathered up the soggy mess, trod on the foot pedal of the bin and threw it all in. Movement in her peripheral vision made her freeze.

A trick of the light...or something else.

The movement continued.

Something else.

She wanted to run away screaming, but despite her fear, Lucy remained still. She held her breath and cautiously slid her eyes sideways toward the mirror. It showed the back of someone's head, exactly as she'd witnessed a few minutes earlier. As she watched, the head turned slowly toward her and revealed the face of Bodie Rodgers, he was staring straight at her. Lucy was struck glacial with fright.

The boy walked away, another figure came into view, a man, a white cane in one hand and the boy's wrist held firmly in the other. Lucy could not pull her eyes away from the unfolding scene. The boy and the blind man walked across a busy road through traffic to a bus stop. In the background Lucy saw several old red brick buildings hidden among a multitude of broad-leafed trees. Near the bus stop, was an arrow sign which pointed down the road, inscribed on it were the words, Historic Navy Yard. Just then Bus 69 arrived, the man and boy got on, followed by several other passengers. Once they were all on board the bus juddered into life and shimmied away out of sight. The mirror steamed over, Lucy's legs collapsed beneath her, she wanted to scream but her mouth was dry with fear. She tried to grab the side of the tub to steady herself, her hand slipped on the wet rim, her head hit the edge and Lucy descended into darkness.

FIVE

'Malloy, phone.' The cop gestured to Malloy through the half open door. 'It's about the boy.'

Malloy grabbed his recently acquired department smart phone from his desk, it showed an incoming call but there was no sound. He looked around the edge for the narrow slit and tried with his thumb then his index finger to flick the tiny horizontal bar.

'Damn these sausages,' he hissed.

The female officer on the next desk held out her hand. 'Give it here.' Malloy took no notice, she snatched it from him, turned off silent mode and passed it back.

'Dinosaur.' She said, shaking her head.

Officer Malloy looked at the screen, it showed an interdepartmental call. He wondered whether to talk to it in his palm like the kids did or put it to his ear, old-school. He pressed the home button and chose the latter.

'Malloy.'

'We got a call, a woman who claims she knows the whereabouts of the missing kid'.

'Another nut job?' Malloy sighed and perched one butt cheek on his desk.

'Says she witnessed him get on a bus, near the Navy Yard, with a blind man, white guy, bus was going to…to Greenwood Park.

'Blind?'

'Yeah, blind, he'd got a white stick, you know one of those with the thing on the end.'

Malloy thought for a second.

'Can we get records of registered blind people who live in the vicinity?

'I guess so.'

'Get me a list and er the witness's address.' Malloy hoped this would be the lead they were looking for.

***

Lucy opened her door. Outside was a police officer. He was tall with dark hair, his nose had been badly broken and by the look of it, on more than one occasion. His skin was scarred from acne and there was not a single place on his cheeks, temples or jawline that didn't resemble the surface of a golf ball. His eyes did all they could to compensate for his unfortunate features, the whites were like Thassos marble, and the irises scintillated pure aquamarine. Lucy had never seen real eyes that colour, she couldn't image they'd be contacts, he didn't look like the type.

'C-can I help you officer…?'

'Malloy, yes you can. Are you…' he looked at his phone screen. 'Miss Sofia Lu…'

'Lucia Randazzo, yes, I'm Lucy.'

'Have you got a moment?' He placed the phone back in his duty belt.

'Yes, sure, sure come on in.' She led him through to the living room and gestured to the least worn seat, for him to sit.

'I guess, I offer you a drink…is that usual or just a thing they do in movies?'

Malloy grinned.

'I'm good, but thanks.'

His phone rang, he patted his jacket pockets one by one.

'Belt.' Lucy pointed out.

Malloy ripped open the pocket on his duty belt and took out the phone. Too late, it fell quiet.

'One moment, please.' He smiled at Lucy and then poked at the home button several times with his index finger. Nothing happened. He looked at Lucy apologetically.

'Maybe a different finger?' Lucy suggested.

Malloy tried with several digits and finally his middle right finger did the trick.

'New issue.' He raised the phone to her, then peered at the screen as if he were doing some complex math.

'That, then that and scroll and...oh! and... recent...and...done!' After getting the right combination, he put the phone to his ear.

'It's Malloy, you called?...He has?...Where?... Uh huh, ok, I will...the what?...No get Hicks to do it.'

He put the phone away.

'Well, I needn't have bothered you.' He stood to leave. 'The boys been found, safe.'

'Oh, that's great news.' Lucy followed him out of the room.

'He wasn't abducted, Musta' been a different kid' He opened the door.

'Different kid?'

'Yeah, the kid you saw, must've been a different kid.' His phone rang again. He opened a pocket, it was empty. Lucy pointed to the one which contained the phone.

'Ugh, yeah gonna take a while to get used to.' Malloy grinned undoing his pocket flap, he got out his phone and stepped into the corridor.

Lucy watched him walk away toward the stairwell, nodding her head appreciatively as she stared at his ass.

SIX

Two lamps made from scaffold poles and old car parts bookended the riveted metal plates which formed the length of the bar at TEXMEX 909. The only other light sources where the candle flames which danced erratically in little colored jars on each table and the hazy nicotine glow of the amber stage lights which bathed Crazee Joe and the Manatees as they pounded out 'Money for Nothing.' at the far side of the diner.

'Maybe get a blister on your…little finger.' Lucy sang rounding it off with a hiccough.

'Maybe get a blister on your thumb.' Chorused her friends.

'You had enough yet Luce?' Slurred Lucy's orange faced friend as she lifted her glass.

'Never Kit, never.'

'That's the way you do it, money for nothing and your kids for free.' Chimed the other friend.

'Kids for free!' Lucy spat out beer, banged down her glass and accidentally knocked Kits drink into her lap. Kit jumped up and surveyed the frothy bubbles as they popped on her jeans.

Then just as suddenly, she sat down again. 'Guy checking us out, guy checking us out, look.' She nodded toward the bar. The others followed her eye-line.

'Yeah mamma,' kit looked on salaciously as the hunk continued to stare in their direction.

Lucy thought she recognised him but couldn't think where from.

The guy moved into a swirl of light to pick up his drink and Kit caught a clearer view of his face.

'Oo, shit, not so much.' She circled her face with her index finger and stuck her tongue out in disgust.

To Kits surprise, Lucy stood and waved.

'Officer Malloy,' Lucy bounded through the chicane of tables over to the bar. 'Am I under surveillance?' She punched his shoulder playfully. 'I've never seen you here before.'

Malloy pointed toward the stage.

'Retired colleague of mine, he's the drummer. First gig, so I said I'd come see him.'

'Cool, come and join us, I know it's a few weeks late but maybe I can get you that drink now?'

Without waiting for an answer, she grabbed his sleeve and dragged him back to her table.

'This is…' She shouted, over the music. 'Officer Malloy.'

Malloy looked around, hoping no one heard the word 'Officer'.

'Malloy, just Malloy.' He nodded at the two women.

'Well, Just-Malloy, these reprobates are my friends, the one with…'

The band blared out Born in the USA, Lucy raised her voice above the cacophony and gestured to Kit. 'The one with the bad orange tan, is Kit and…'

'Hey, it's meant to look this way.'

'You mean you actually wanna look like an Oompah Loompa, or are ya tryin to attract one for a date?'

'At least I can get a date.' Kit said defensively.

'What?' Lucy cocked her ear toward Kit.

'At least I can get a date.' Kit shouted.

'What?' Lucy cocked her ear again and grinned.

Kit flipped her the finger as Lucy circled the table.

'And this is Jaz. My *best* friend.' She glanced sidelong at Kit before pecking Jaz's cheek and snuggling her head on her shoulder.

'Dyke.' Kit said with a smirk.

'Look who's talking!' Lucy contracted her chin back toward her neck and opened her eyes wide. 'Miss, found in bed with another woman.'

'I was drunk and high and she looked like a guy.' Kit retorted as she fabricated a look of innocence on her pumpkin-coloured face.

'Oh, and a poet too.' Lucy countered.

'Would you ladies like a drink or something to eat maybe?' Malloy said, hoping to divert the conversation.

The women's attention was instantly gained. Malloy gestured to a string bean of a waitress, who hurried over to take their food and beverage order.

An hour later, stomachs full and all the usual chit chat done, they sat and listened to the band play their final song.

Malloy turned to Lucy 'You wanna dance?'

'Er, yeah, sure, ok.'

He took her hand and she noticed there was no wedding ring on his finger, as they got to the dance floor Malloy slunk his arms around Lucy's waist she reciprocated, sliding her hands up to his shoulders and interlacing her fingers behind his neck. Kit and Jazz looked at each other in disbelief.

'Lay lady lay, lay on my big brass bed.' Malloy crooned.

'You don't waste time do you.' Lucy looked past the rocks of his face, into his eyes.

'No!' He hastily stepped away from her. 'No, I was, I was just singing along, I didn't mean…it wasn't a…'

Lucy jabbed him in the stomach. 'Gotcha.' She said and logged that there was nothing soft about his belly. It was taut, either he was wearing a girdle, or he worked out, she suppressed a giggle, pulled him close and placed her head on his shoulder. He smelled good too.

They danced a slow dance for several minutes before Lucy was overwhelmed with a desire to ask about the missing boy.

'So, the little guy was ok?'

'Eh?' Malloy looked at her quizzically.

Lucy leant nearer his ear. 'The missing boy, you said he'd not been taken, what happened, he run away or somethin?'

The music quietened then stopped, they clapped their appreciation along with rest of the audience and Malloy gave a manly wave to his drummer friend, who in turn lifted a drumstick to his forehead in mock salute.

The band began to leave the stage. Nearby a

table of intoxicated guys began to chant.

'Aero…smith…Aero…smith…'

'Ok guys, ok.' The singer gestured for them to pipe down. 'Hows about a little, Love in an elevator!' He said addressing the band as well as the audience. Wearily the musicians returned to their instruments, whoops came from the crowd and the band sprung into life for an encore.

Malloy grabbed Lucy's hand and the two wended their way through the tables to the far end of the bar, Lucy glanced over to Kit and Jazz, they were no longer at the table but were dancing raucously with the drunken Aerosmith fans.

When they reached the quieter part of the bar, Malloy let go of Lucy's hand and turned to her.

'You were right.'

'About what?'

'The boy and the blind guy.'

'The blind guy took him?'

'No, no he wasn't taken by the blind guy, he was the one took the blind guy!'

'What?' Lucy was confused.

'The boy wanted to go to some art installation at the Greenwood cemetery, something about posting a note to his dead mom, he used the blind guy to get on the bus, clever kid, knew that way he wouldn't get questioned about his age.'

Lucy stiffened, a washing drum heavy with water and linens turned laboriously in her stomach as she realised the mirror was right.

Malloy paused. 'You ok? You look a weird color.'

'No, I'm fine, just...er, gas you know from the chilli.' She cringed inwardly...*Oh crap, I've just told him I've got gas, guess it's better than saying I saw the boy in a magic mirror. But why'd I have to say gas!*

'Seems he got lost on the way back and scared, spent the night way over at Creek Park, poor kid. Next day he tried to get a bus home with no money, driver wouldn't let him board on his own.' Malloy shrugged his shoulders and scratched the back of his neck. 'I guess there's only so many blind people around.' He laughed.

The band played their last notes to a scatter of applause.

Lucy stared at Malloy blankly, she thought about the mirror back at her apartment.

'You sure you're ok?' Malloy put his hand on her shoulder.

Her answer wasn't heard above the voices of her friends as they chorused...

'Malloy and Lucy, sittin' in a tree K.I.S.S.'

Lucy swung round, Jaz and Kit sat chins on wrists, leering over the backs of their chairs.

'.S.S.I.N,' Jaz continued.

'How many S's?' Kit said sneering at Jaz.

'I'm drunk.' Jaz took a gulp of her drink.

'Ladies, ladies.' Lucy gained their attention. 'Shut the fuck up and mind your own damn business.'

'Nice.' Kit screwed up her face, leant across and whispered to Jaz, the two turned simultaneously and smirked at Lucy.

'Well.' Malloy interrupted. 'I gotta get to work.'

'Oh.' Lucy said with an accidental tone of disappointment, which she instantly regretted.

Malloy smiled. 'I guess we could…another…?'

'Sure.' Lucy walked away quickly, hoping to leave behind the uncommon feeling of vulnerability which had popped up on her unexpectedly. 'You know where I'm at…Officer Malloy.' She waved her hand above her head nonchalantly, not bothering to turn round. She had an inkling if she got involved with this guy, he'd want to be more than a friend with benefits and what was worse, what scared her more, was the idea appealed.

Lucy sat with the girls at the table, her salivary glands tingling, like the first time she'd had tequila and the first time she'd met Tom.

Why this guy, he's got a great physique sure and

there is something in his eyes more than the crazy blue colour, something, something, oh hell.

She turned; Malloy was gone. She grabbed her beer and took a large gulp, as she swallowed, the mirror slipped back into her thoughts. Without a word to her chattering friends, Lucy grabbed her jacket, sidled away from the table, out of the club and into the night.

SEVEN

It was the first time Lucy had been scared to enter her apartment. She stood in the stair well, took a breath of bravery, turned the key in the lock and stepped inside. A cold stagnant quality hit her, along with a feeling of foreboding, it inched its way from the skin on her shins up to the centre of her chest. Behind her the door creaked to a close, adding an eerie gravitas to the moment. She peeled off her jacket and flung it through the living room doorway toward the couch, it didn't quite reach, instead it perched momentarily, saddle-like across the back, before sliding slowly to the floor. Ignoring it she walked to the bathroom further down the hall.

What shall I ask it…what's the winning Lottery numbers, who's gonna win the Super Bowl?

She stared at the door for a moment.

The boy was lost, maybe I should try and find something I've lost?

She thought of the necklace, a birthday gift from Tom. A white-gold chain bearing a snowflake pendant, set with melee diamonds.

'Ok, let's do this.' She said steeling herself as she opened the bathroom door. The mirror was on the windowsill, doing what mirrors do best and reflecting, it looked no more intimidating than the hairbrush lying next to it.

Lucy's heart thumped against her ribcage as she stepped through the doorway and walked toward the mirror, her head pulsing with lava hot blood as she reached out and took it from the shelf, her image in the glass ballooned as she lifted it to her eye-line and searched its reflections, its cold cylindrical neck fit snuggly into her palm.

She closed her eyes and thought hard about her missing necklace, after a few seconds she opened her right eye, the mirror showed her face, her hair, the floor behind her, a shadow on the shower curtain, the crack in the ceiling. Nothing unusual. She opened her other eye, flipped over the mirror and scrutinised the back, not having the faintest idea what she was looking for. Finding nothing she flipped it over again. That's when she saw a silvery glint reflected in the glass, sliding its way past the door frame. She spun quickly. But it had disappeared.

She looked back into the mirror and like the 'glitch cat' in the Matrix, the silvery white tail of the chain slipped once again, out of the door. She checked in the hallway and found nothing. Shakily she returned the mirror to its place on the sill and covered it with a towel. Her stomach began to cramp, she pressed one hand hard against it, the other against her mouth, she needed to be out of there. Turning round and round so nothing could creep up on her, she left the room, barely able to keep a lid on the panic ping ponging around in her chest. Once in the hall she walked backward toward the kitchen breathing heavily, worked herself through the door, shut it, sat down on a kitchen stool, and stared at the door handle.

What the hell next?

EIGHT

6am, Malloy received a call. An early morning jogger discovered a body at Crotona Park, his was the nearest patrol car. He flicked on the top lights, pushed his foot down on the accelerator and sped off, much to the annoyance of his partner Cable who was trying to drink his last coffee of the nightshift.

Several minutes later Malloy took a right on to Claremont parkway which led through the centre of Crotona Park. Halfway down he turned into a short drive stopping by a gap in the hip high wooden fence. The witness was nowhere to be seen; his morning run obviously more important than what remained of a lifeless human being.

The trees here were at their most dense, but despite their foliage throwing dark confusing shadows upon the coarse grass, it didn't take more than a minute for Malloy to locate the body.

Whoever did this wanted it to be found. Malloy looked down at the woman, she was face up prostrate in the short grass.

'We got another one.' He shouted, turning to Cable who was fumbling about in the trunk of the patrol car. 'Same M.O. as before.'

This woman, like the previous two, was missing her lips, they'd been sliced away and replaced by a single line of industrial staples which pinned the remnants of tattered skin to her gums. Malloy looked closer and saw short strands of red hair sticking out from between the metal strips and her shattered teeth. He noted too that most of her hair, like the other victims, was wet with red dye, he could see she'd previously been blonde as some of her roots remained untouched. There were several thick patches of dried black blood where sections of hair had been yanked from her scalp. Malloy knew from experience she'd been alive when it happened. He wondered what had become of her lips, then imagined the loved ones they'd kissed. He gulped and swallowed down his anger.

'Fuck me, look at that.' Cable leant across Malloy and flicked over a Zippo lighter with the toe of his shoe. 'You don't see many like that anymore.'

Malloy stuck his arm out to halt Cable.

'Hey! That's evidence and show some respect.'

Cable retracted his foot.

'It's a passion of mine, drives the wife crazy.' He stared a little closer at the object. 'Looks broke anyhow.' He said ending with a tut. Cable looked up and beamed at Malloy.

'I've got some worth hundreds of dollars you know.' He didn't wait for an answer. 'I'm gonna build some display cabinets in the den and…'

Cable's chat about Zippo lighters faded into a monotonous mumble.

Malloy took out his pad and began to write notes, nodding every now and then, just to be polite. He paused as he remembered he was due to take a training module the following week, on how to use the app on his new phone, to keep records, instead of the outdated pocketbooks. Technology wasn't his strong point; the younger cops knew it and regularly busted his balls about his lack of knowledge in that area.

Once the scene was stabilised, Cable began to cordon off the area around the body, all the time lecturing about his hoard of collectible lighters.

Within fifteen minutes the previously quiet Crotona Park was alive with flashing lights. Other officers arrived followed by the crime scene unit and medical examiner. Malloy knew he was in for a tough end to his shift, but on the positive side, he knew more about Zippo lighters than he did an hour ago.

NINE

Lucy stared at her kitchen door until the need for coffee outweighed her fear of what happened in the bathroom earlier. This mirror business was serious shit, only the real stuff would do, so she ground some Arabica beans, made herself a strong coffee and a pastrami sandwich, placed everything on a tray and went through the hall to her living room, steering well clear of the bathroom as she went. Positioning herself on the couch facing the door to the hall she mulled over what she'd seen in the mirror and tried to figure out what it meant. Although it was late, she no longer felt like sleeping, partly to do with the amount of coffee she'd consumed and partly due to the feeling of unease and vulnerability which shrouded her.

She turned on the T.V. there was a rerun of a comedy series she'd not watched in years, something funny would help take her mind off the current situation.

Just after 6am Lucy woke with a stiff neck, aching back and a desperate need to urinate. She stood shakily, swayed into the hall, flicked on the light, and braced herself against the jamb before pushing open the bathroom door. She was relieved to see there was nothing amiss, she pulled down her cargos and underwear and squatted above the toilet. After peeing as quickly as possible, she washed and dried her hands and gave her teeth a perfunctory brush. As she rinsed out her toothbrush, a thought crossed her mind. Quickly she tied her hair with a band, removed the towel from the mirror and took it into the hallway. The previous night she'd been able to see the vision of the necklace only when looking through the mirror. Maybe the necklace was so close she just needed to use the mirror like a divining rod, follow it's reflected image and see where it went. She tilted the mirror toward the floor.

'Show me my necklace, where is it?' Her voice, too loud and nervous, made her cringe. She braced herself and, in the time it took to open her eyes from a blink, an image appeared in the mirror. Lucy fought to keep her breathing steady, she watched in the glass as the reflection of the silver strand slinked along the hall floor, it wasn't an exact replica of her lost necklace, it was more like a suggestion of it. She walked steadily backward making sure she kept the mirror in a position to be able to view the silver thread, she followed it to her bedroom door where it stopped momentarily before skittering through the gap underneath. Lucy balanced on one leg and pushed the door open with the sole of her other foot. The door swung wide, she backed into the room twisting the mirror trying to find where the thread went, then to her horror she glimpsed a tiny spark disappear beneath her bed.

'Yeah, course that's where you're gonna go, great.' Lucy desperately tried to think of a film where going under the bed to follow something weird, had ever turned out well. She ducked and swerved in an attempt to view another glint in the mirror, but there was none. For several minutes she stood and stared at the bed knowing what she must do, but not relishing it one bit. Putting the mirror down on her nightstand she knelt and looked carefully under her bed for a sign of any strange swirling blackness, red eyes, taloned hands, or sharp teeth that may be ready to grab or bite her. Thankfully there was nothing but a few sleeping dust bunnies and a screwed-up tissue.

Which part to slide under first, she pondered, feet or head. She decided the safest way was to lay flat on her back on the floor and glide under sideways. So laying down on the cool wood laminate she slid herself along by pulling on the slats on the underside of the bed, the movement from her body caused the dust bunnies to swirl. Skin flakes, dust mite faeces and other detritus became airborne. Lucy's nose tickled, and as particles coalesced inside her nostrils, she tilted back her head in a pre-sneeze inhalation…and she saw it. Her necklace, the real necklace, dangling from either side of a bed slat, just above her right temple.

I've found it, no, the mirror has found it.

The sneeze arrived powerful and undeniable. Lucy's head hurtled forward, thwacked against the wooden slats and for the second time that week she saw stars.

***

There's never anything I can do, once it's started, I know they understand that. Yet they still plead with me.

'Why me?'
'Why are you doing this?'

'Please don't'

'I promise I won't tell.'

I've heard it all before, I hate them for it. Hate the way they talk, like the actors on a TV crime show. Has no-one got anything original to say anymore? People are lazy. It's the moms who are to blame, sitting watching reality TV, drinking, taking drugs and prostituting themselves in the pursuit of love, whilst their kids get screwed over by life. They chose to have the kids, so why the hell don't they love them enough to save them? If they won't bleed for their children...

He carefully placed the lips into the container of borax and shook it gently so they were covered in the white powder.

...then I'll make sure they bleed for me.

Ten

'Do you want me to hit you over the head and make it three times?' Chinah laughed as she studied the bruise on Lucy's forehead. 'It's getting a bit of a habit, knocking yaself out.'

Lucy arranged her hair over the purple line left by the wooden bed slat and opened a binder on her desk. 'I only knocked myself out the first time.' She stated matter-of-factly.

'So, you're telling me, this magic mirror told you about the lost boy *and* where your necklace was?' Chinah said raising an eyebrow.

'Yeah, No…well it reflected, it didn't like, speak to me.' Lucy sat down at her computer and turned it on.

'Oh, weeeeeell that's ok then, cos if it spoke to you that *would* be crazy.' Chinah added a derisive snort to emphasise her disbelief. 'You shoulda seen a doctor when you hit the tub side, and now you're telling me you hit ya damn head… again. You know people die, they D.I.E days after having a bump like you got, go…see…a doctor.' She made to leave the room, then stopped and turned back to Lucy.

'What now?' Lucy rolled her eyes. 'Surely you've work you should be doing?'

Chinah didn't answer, she laid her copy of the New York Wire on top of Lucy's paperwork and flicked through a few pages. 'Maybe if it could find this guy, I might believe your freaky ass story.' She prodded at the copy.

Lucy followed Chinah's finger and read aloud.

Third body found.
Lead investigators are linking the murder of Jada Redmond, single mother of three, to another two bodies found with similar identifying…

'Then you and this wacko could maybe get together and go see the same shrink.' Chinah concluded.

Lucy rolled up the newspaper and held it in the air threateningly. Chinah poked out her tongue.

'Fuck you Chinah Ross!' Lucy tried not to laugh as she jabbed the paper towards her colleague's face. 'Anyhow, who said it's a guy?'

Chinah batted at the newspaper hard enough for it to fly from Lucy's hand and made a break for the door.

'It's always a guy.' She said, trotting from the room.

Lucy pursued her to the open doorway and shouted down the corridor. 'You're buying me lunch dipshit.'

***

Three days after Lucy and Chinah's conversation an article appeared in the New York Wire.

Manhattan woman helps find lost boy with 'Magic Mirror.'

Chinah read it gleefully to Lucy at work that morning.

Lucy's name was mentioned and so was the story about her necklace. All the information was slightly exaggerated, something Lucy put down to Chinah's embellishments.

'What the hell,' Lucy strode toward Chinah. 'You've no right to go and give that story to the press, I'll be a laughing stock, you stupid stupid assho…'. She stopped short as their boss barged through the door, shaking a copy of the paper.

'Is this true?'

'No, no…' Lucy chewed her lip. '…well, yes.' She shrugged her shoulders not knowing quite what to say.

'You think you can find my wife and that damn hillbilly she ran off with?'

'I, Erm…seriously?' Lucy glanced at Chinah for some sort of reference as to how she should answer, but Chinah avoided eye contact.

'No, of course not.' He flared. 'Don't be an idiot, get back to work both of you.' He pointed to each of them in turn with the rolled-up newspaper. Then jabbed it toward Lucy 'Don't let me ever see your name in here again unless it's in the obituaries.' He flung the paper at her. 'Thank God you weren't stupid enough to mention where you work.' He left the room slamming the door behind him.

'Chinah, I could've lost my job, you stupid dumbass!'

'Doubt it, you're the shining star of Maniac Locations.' Chinah replied haughtily. 'You'd have to take a dump on the boss's desk before he'd fire you. You got your name in the Wire, I don't see what you're so upset about.' She picked up the paper from the floor, folded it with the one she already carried and left the room.

Lucy sat down at her computer and contemplated what had just transpired. Then on impulse picked up her phone, scrolled for a number and tapped it.

'Hi…I need to speak to Officer Malloy…Sofia-Lucia Randazzo, just tell him it's Lucy.

***

He picked up the book of matches, flicked it open, lit one and held it to his cigarette. The woman's constant yawping in the next room really got under his skin. He inhaled the beauty of the nicotine into his lungs, felt it fire into his arteries and send a buzz round his head. Three days this time, God he wished he could quit. The woman in the other room blubbered. He smiled and picked up the staple gun from the counter. Cigarette break over. He took a last draw, threw the butt on the ground and crunched it beneath his boot. Time to get back to work.

ELEVEN

'I'm glad you could meet me, would meet me.' Lucy pulled out a chair in the tiny bistro and settled opposite Malloy.

'I was gonna call you, and then…' Malloy's voice trailed off.

'And then you saw the article and decided I was a whack job; I don't blame you.' She signalled to the waiter to bring her the same beer as Malloy. 'I wanna ask you something and you can say no if you want and that'll be the end of it.'

Malloy leant his forearms on the table and wrapped his hands around his beer.

'Ok, you've poked at my curiosity.'

Lucy adjusted herself nervously in her seat, twiddled with her bottom lip, then interlaced her fingers and leant toward Malloy. She spoke as if she were calming a child, quiet and even.

'Just say, for instance that there *was* such a

thing as a magical mirror.' She watched Malloy stiffen and his eyes widen slightly.

'I know, I know it's crazy, but bear with me.' She paused as the waiter set down her beer and asked if they were ready to order food. Malloy told him to give them a minute and when the waiter had gone Lucy continued, more upbeat this time. 'If you inherited a mirror, that could seemingly do…magical stuff.'

Lucy felt her face redden, sweat beaded on her forehead, she couldn't quite believe what she was saying. She gulped and continued. 'And you weren't sure if you were going mad or if it did possess some strange ability, wouldn't you want someone else to check it out?' She rubbed her clammy palms together and watched Malloy's face. His perfect eyes were steely and unblinking.

'I guess.' He shrugged his shoulders and took a quick swig of his beer.

'And wouldn't you want that somebody to be impartial and trustworthy?'

Malloy's face went blank. Lucy felt she was losing him.

'Ok,' She sat up straight and placed her fists purposely on the tabletop. 'Let's say I cook you dinner at mine. Whilst you're there you take a little look at the mirror, you know, like, just a little ole mirror and if it *is* just a mirror and I'm crazy, then walk away.' She fanned out her fingers and sat back. 'You're a big guy, you can take care of yourself. No harm done and you get a free meal.'

'Yeah, but with a crazy woman.' Malloy narrowed his eyes in contemplation and stared at Lucy for a few seconds before reaching for his beer. 'You vegetarian?' He said lifting his glass to his lips.

'No, definitely not.' Lucy shook her head vigorously.

'Then it's a deal.' Malloy took a few gulps of beer and placed the bottle down with purpose. 'So?'

Lucy cocked her head to one side. 'So, what?'

'Are you ready?'

'Now?'

'Why not? I may change my mind by tomorrow, strike whilst the irons hot I say.' He stood and turned to the waiter who was resetting a table.

'Hey, buddy, we'll catch you next time.' The waiter looked a little confused. 'Emergency.' Malloy raised both his hands and shrugged his shoulders apologetically. The waiter nodded his understanding. Malloy placed some bills on the table and walked outside, closely followed by Lucy.

'If you want me to cook, then we gotta shop.' She pointed to the Deli-grocery a few doors away on the corner of Vermilyea and Academy.

Lucy remembered she'd some left-over potatoes in the refrigerator, fried up with some greens, salt, pepper and garlic they'd be just fine.

At the deli she picked up some snow peas and chose a couple of steaks from the chill counter.

'You want beer?' She asked Malloy.

Malloy thought for a second.

'Yeah, Dutch courage.' His eyes sparkled fiercely above a wry grin. 'Maybe a couple of packs?'

'I like your thinking.' Lucy picked up two six packs. Malloy took them from her.

'My treat.'

'Aw, aren't you mister polite.'

They paid, left the store, and continued up Academy toward Seaman Avenue, for a while they walked quietly side by side, until finally Lucy broke the silence.

'I erm, noticed the other night you weren't wearing a wedding ring.' She studied the sidewalk as she spoke.

'Three years clean.' He laughed. 'No, I, I'm divorced.'

'You don't seem too sure.' Lucy glanced at him sideways.

'I guess I'm still not over her.'

Lucy felt a ripple of shock, she'd taken him for a tough guy. But maybe that was because he looked like he should be.

'Mel, my wife, she wanted kids as soon as we got married, like young idiots we'd never really discussed it. I figured we'd have more time together first, then when I gave in, I found my, my guys were…not viable…anyway we tried a lot of stuff that didn't work, then she was all for donors and adoption and stuff. But if I was gonna have any, kids I mean, I wanted one that was mine, y'know. We argued, well she argued, I stuck my head in the sand. After a while we stopped talking about it, I thought we were okay, then a few years later I discovered she was seeing her ex.'

'She left you then?' Lucy asked gently.

'Nah. She'd no intention of leaving me, she was in it for a baby, he was in it for the sex. She was four months gone before I found out about the affair. We fought, she…she…'

Lucy put her hand on his shoulder.

'It's ok, you don't need to tell me'.

Malloy shook his head, Lucy sensed he needed to finish the roller coaster ride, despite the obvious pain it caused him.

'We fought, I was…crazy, angry, I pushed her, thought she'd land softly on the couch.' He lowered his head 'I didn't know she was learning to knit, y'know things for the baby…I didn't see the…' He stopped and looked away from Lucy. 'The baby didn't make it.'

'Oh my God, I'm so sorry.'

'It's ok, it's ok.' He walked on. 'Mel recovered, she lives with an anaesthesiologist, in Tribeca, they got three kids, two adopted, one of their own, I visit sometimes.'

'No, I meant, sorry for you.' Lucy touched his forearm.

'I'm ok.' He forced a smile. 'Isn't this your place.' He gestured to the building.

Lucy was impressed he'd remembered.

'Sure is.' She fumbled in her pocket for her keys. Opened the door and walked inside. Then realised Malloy wasn't following. She looked back at him.

'You coming?'

Malloy put the bags of groceries down on the sidewalk. 'Just checking the building, if you turn out to be a crazy knife wielding bitch, I need to know the quickest way out.'

'Seriously, hand on heart.' She placed her hand

where she thought her heart was. 'I promise, I'm only two of those things.'

Malloy picked up the bags and followed her inside.

After climbing several flights of stairs, they arrived at the door to Lucy's apartment, entered and went down the narrow hallway to the kitchen. Lucy got the pea pods from the bag, put them into a steamer, took the potatoes from the refrigerator and set about frying the steaks.

'Wow, you really know how to get a meal started.' Malloy said incredulously.

Lucy turned to see him staring at the grey potatoes.

'You sure they're ok?' He shook the container, sniffed the contents suspiciously and not detecting any strange odour returned them to the counter.

'Yeah, they're fine, just get the grater out.' Lucy pointed to the kitchen unit next to Malloy. 'There's garlic in that pot, grate two cloves over the potatoes add some salt and pepper and then pass them here.'

Malloy stalled for a moment to take in what she'd said.

'Quickly, they're nearly done. I'm doing the steaks bloody. No arguments, they shouldn't be eaten any other way.' Lucy flipped the tranches of meat one at a time, then watched patiently as Malloy completed his task.

He handed her the bowl containing the potato concoction and Lucy threw it in the pan alongside the steaks. It sizzled sending a pungent smell of garlic through the air. Malloy took a seat and watched Lucy pat the mixture for a few minutes with the convex side of a wooden spoon. She scooped the steaks onto plates, then flipped over the rapidly browning mixture in the pan to let it heat through on the other side. The steamer pinged and minutes later they sat at the table eating hungrily and swilling down a beer each.

'You weren't wrong.' Malloy mumbled. He lifted some of the potato mixture onto his fork, pointed to it and gave a thumbs up. He swallowed the previous mouthful and immediately stuffed the loaded fork into his mouth.

'Jesus, when did you last have a meal?' Lucy gaped at him as fork-load after fork-load disappeared.

'I get things on the fly mostly, not often I have a meal cooked for me.' He looked up out of the top right corner of his eye searching for a memory.

'Three years ago.'

'What! That's crazy.' Lucy lifted her beer to her lips and anticipated the liquid, but it was empty.

She peered at it in annoyance.

'More beer' she said rhetorically, as she lifted the bottle above her head.

Malloy stood, collected the plates, placed them onto the counter and turned on the faucet.

Lucy watched him as she got two bottles from the freezer compartment, where she'd put them for a quick chill.

'Have we got this the wrong way round?' She tilted her head and smiled.

'It's twenty nineteen, not nineteen twenty, didn't you girls fight for this right.' Malloy sank the dishes into the frothy water and swished them about.

'Girls, who you callin' girls?' Lucy placed the beers on the table and walked to where Malloy stood with sudsy hands.

'Besides we *girls* got dishwashers.' She opened the door next to Malloys thigh.

'Ah, ok.' He shook the bubbles off one of the dishes and went to place it in the dishwasher.

Lucy took it from him, pulled out a rack from inside and arranged the plate in one of the slots.

'Leave it, I'll do it later, I got a system.'

'You got a system?' He teased.

'Yeah, I got a system.' Lucy closed the dishwasher door, turned and leant back against the counter; she was incredibly close to Malloy. So close she could feel the soft hairs on his arm touch her wrist. In order to move her hand away surreptitiously, she brushed back her hair, it was knotty, and her fingers stuck in the tangles. To her surprise Malloy grabbed her round the waist and pulled her to him. She took a sharp breath in as he pushed a kiss onto her lips. He immediately released her, sliding away before she could reciprocate.

'Some things I still do the old way.' He said, giving Lucy a lopsided grin. He picked up his beer and walked into the hall. 'C'mon, I s'pose you'd better show me this fantastical mirror before we forget…' he snorted a little laugh. 'Like we'd forget that.'

Lucy followed him into the hallway, opened the bathroom door with ceremony and indicated for him to go inside. Malloy looked around the room.

'This it?' He pointed to a mirror on the windowsill.

'No.' Lucy removed a towel from the shelf next to the bathroom cabinet, the mirror was face down beneath it. 'It's this one.' She handed it to Malloy.

'Ah yes, more like what you'd imagine a magic mirror to look like.' He studied all sides of the object, shook his head and laughed. 'What the hell did I just say.' He positioned the mirror in front of the modern square one on the sill. 'Crazy, isn't catching, is it?' He stood back from the window and looked at Lucy blankly. 'Now what?'

'Now we have to find something.' She glanced around the bathroom then back at Malloy. 'What you got in your pocket?'

Malloy fumbled around and brought out a rabbit's foot keychain and dangled it in front of Lucy's face.

'Will this do?'

'Good as anything.' She gestured to the hall. 'Now go and hide it somewhere.'

'Really, we seriously doing this, sure you don't want to stop now and save your embarrassment?'

'We're really doing this.' Lucy turned him round and shoved him in the back.

Malloy stumbled out the room. Lucy listened to him pacing around the apartment.

'Mm nice panties.' He called from the bedroom.

'Shit.' Lucy hissed under her breath. Then shouted. 'Keep your damn mind on the task officer.'

A few seconds later Malloy stepped back into the bathroom and sat on the edge of the tub.

'Ready?' Lucy tucked her hair behind her ears.

'Ready.' Malloy replied, his eyes twinkling in amusement.

Lucy turned and faced the mirror, her back to Malloy.

'Where is Malloy's key chain?' She waited and watched her reflection, thirty seconds passed, nothing happened. She turned to Malloy. 'Bear with me.' She turned back and addressed the mirror again.

'Where is Malloy's rabbit foot key chain?'

Still nothing. Malloy cleared his throat noisily. Lucy shot him a pissed look, then turned back to the mirror, it was steaming over like before, Lucy's stomach spasmed into knots as she watched swirls of grey cover the whole of the glass and slowly darken to black.

'Mm it's somewhere dark.' She mused.

'Oh my God you're amazing.' Malloy laughed sarcastically, as he wondered where she'd purchased this trick mirror. He stood up and peered at it over Lucy's shoulder.

'Shit.' They shouted simultaneously as the rabbit's foot image appeared in the mirror, surrounded by fingers.

Malloy took his hand out of his pocket and threw the rabbits foot across the room in fright.

They both turned to bolt from the room, got stuck in the doorway momentarily, like they were in a Stooges skit, then ran through the hall to the far side of the kitchen.

Lucy began to laugh hysterically.

'I told you; I fucking told you it could find things.'

'No, shit.' Malloy panted.

TWELVE

Cable opened the plastic container he'd got balanced on his lap, the air in the patrol car instantly became tinged with the sweet smell of cloves, ginger and cinnamon.

'Carole's made you cookies.' Cable turned the container toward Malloy, took one out and devoured it.

'Wow, am I gonna get some this time?' Malloy snatched one from the box, crammed it into his mouth and quickly took another.

'You've been quiet tonight, what's wrong?' Cable mumbled, crumbs rolling down his shirt.

'When'd you become Mr sensitive?' Malloy gave Cable a side on glance.

'Just asking.' Cable replied, batting away the cookie crumbs with the back of his hand. 'You seem tense like you got something wrong with your butt.'

Cable was right, (apart from the bit about his butt), Malloy couldn't stop the bizarre events of the previous evening from repeating over and over in his head. After finding his rabbit's foot, he and Lucy finished the rest of the beers along with a bottle of wine, and in her drunkenness, Lucy suggested asking the mirror about the murders. Question after question, it reflected nothing more than the darkening images in the room, dumfounded they decided to hide random objects around Lucy's apartment in an attempt to see how accurate it was and to their amazement, he and Lucy, or more precisely the mirror, found them all. Exciting as the game was, it left them no wiser as to why the mirror failed to show anything when asked about the killer.

'See, you're just not listening, what's with you tonight?' Cables voice jolted Malloy from his thoughts.

The traffic lights ahead turned red, Malloy slowed to a stop, hastily he grabbed the box of cookies from Cables fingers and stowed it away in the glove compartment. Cable didn't protest, he simply reached behind his seat, brought out a paper bag unfolded the top and pulled out a cookie.

'Emergency supply.' He declared.

The light changed to green. Malloy drove on, his thoughts instantly turning back to the mirror.

What's the common thread, it's not the time of day, Lucy'd asked questions day and night. Position? No, the mirror was always in the bathroom. The things found then? The rabbit's foot's mine, the necklace and all the other items belonged to Lucy, the boy, she'd not known him, nor did she know the murdered women... the boy's picture had been in the paper, the women's had not, damn, nothing makes any sense.

Malloy shook his head and started again.

Everything we found had been Lucy's, except for my rabbit's foot, the boy and the victims. She'd seen all her things, but not any of the others....no, she'd seen the rabbit's foot momentarily. Then it hit him.

She'd seen the boy in the paper, she'd seen the rabbit's foot before he hid it, she'd seen all the rest, but no-one knew what the killer looked like, including Lucy...Shit that's it! She needed to have seen what was lost before it could be found!

He wanted to whoop and slap the steering wheel, but forced himself to internalise the celebration, the last thing he needed was to have Cable asking questions.

For several minutes he wracked his brain and tried to come up with a way to solve the conundrum. Then an idea came to him.

'We gotta go to Dumbo.'

Cable swallowed the last of his cookie.

'Why?' He screwed up the bag and threw it into the footwell.

'Don't think I'm gonna get that!' Malloy pointed at the crumpled mass. 'Jeez you're such a slob.'

Cable picked a crumb from his shirt and popped it into his mouth. 'Why we goin to Dumbo?'

'Just wanna take another look at that evidence from the red dye case.' Malloy lied.

'Uh, kay.' Cable couldn't be bothered to ask why again, anyhow, he needed a leak, and the Johns at Front Street were the cleanest for miles. Besides it was Rosie's night on the desk and whilst Malloy was doing whatever crackpot thing he'd got in mind, Cable decided he'd do himself a little flirting. Rosie was his type, Rebel Wilson pretty, always ready with a dirty joke and a big smile. Her skin was baby pink, plentiful and soft like marshmallow. Cable often imagined getting lost in its luscious folds, maybe tonight would be his opportunity to ask her on a date, he twisted his wedding ring free from his finger and as Malloy took a right toward Brooklyn, Cable surreptitiously concealed it in his pants pocket.

***

Her head and shoulders lay across his thighs. Face upward, she breathed soft and deep. Quiet as a sleeping new-born.

With his right hand he carefully combed the bleach through her hair one last time.

> 'Who ne'er taught this child to play,
> Or love gods holy book or day,
> Who walks in devils' shoes away,
> My Mother.

> And never will she fail to be,
> So wicked and unkind to me,
> There's none so shamed to God as she,
> My mother.'

He rinsed the woman's hair with water from a jug by his side and gently took his hand from her neck, leaving it kinked at an awkward angle, chin jutting upward. He put on the newly powdered latex gloves, squeezed the tube of red dye into his palm, rubbed it between his hands and applied it along the length of her freshly yellowed hair.

E'en the devil can't disguise,
She is the crow with lying eyes,
Whom feasts upon an infants cry.
My Mother.

Calmly, he wrenched a fistful of hair from her scalp, pried open her mouth and shoved in the strands. Her body showed signs that somewhere in her drugged mind she was aware of what was happening, she convulsed, he held her tight and pushed the hair further into her mouth toward her throat.

'Shush, shush.' He whispered ripping a second handful from her scalp. 'In the end, everything will be…just…hunky-dory.'

THIRTEEN

The apartment door buzzer sounded a second time.

'Don't be so damn impatient.' Lucy shouted redundantly, as she pressed the intercom button 'Yes?'

'Lucy it's Malloy.'

'It's seven thirty, what the hell.' She buzzed him in. 'It's open.' Then realising her apartment was in a total mess she quickly ran around, scooping up all the dirty clothes and trash, dashed into her bedroom and piled them onto the dresser. She took a few steps toward the door, turned back, grabbed the pile, threw it to the floor and hurriedly kicked it under the bed.

There was a rapid knocking on the door.

'Ok, I know you're there, no need to bash the damn door in.' Lucy pulled the bolt across and felt Malloy push from the other side. 'Impatient!'

He burst through the door and shoved a Zippo lighter toward her face.

'You know what this is?'

Lucy pulled a face and batted away Malloy's hand. 'It's a Lighter.'

'No, it's a key.' Malloy said triumphantly, closing the door and ushering her down the hall and into the kitchen.

'What?' Lucy took a glass from the cupboard. 'What d'you mean a key?' She put the glass down, and turned to Malloy, he was in the doorway, face beaming with delight.

'A key to finding who the killer is.' He swung the lighter round between his thumb and forefinger.

Lucy walked over, took the Zippo and looked at it quizzically.

Then out of his pocket Malloy produced a silver cover, one he'd borrowed from Cable. 'I reckon what we need to do, is ask where this part.' he held up the cover for Lucy to see, 'of that lighter is.' He took the Zippo out of Lucy's hand and clipped the two parts together. 'You know what it looks like, so the mirror will too.'

'I'm still not with you.' Lucy began. Then suddenly realised what Malloy meant. 'Thats the killers?'

'Could be, it was found next to the body of the last victim.' He placed the lighter on the table and Lucy stared at it in horror. 'I've got an old friend, works in evidence, she owes me a favour, I cleared up a situation with her kid once,'

He placed the lighter on the tabletop, 'but it's gotta go back A, sap.'

'I can't do anything now, I gotta get to work.' Lucy pushed by him, walked down the hall and disappeared into the living room.

'Can you get off early?' Malloy asked following her.

Lucy thought for a few seconds. 'Well, I could go look at a potential set, I guess, it's not far from here.' She pulled on the sleeve of her jacket, checked her keys were in the pocket, put her arm in the other sleeve and left the room. Malloy was waiting for her at the door.

'Meet you there at three.' She flicked her hair out from her collar. 'You can pick me up, I'll text you the address.'

Malloy followed her out of the apartment. 'Ok, that gives me time to get some sleep.' he began to yawn, rubbed his hand around his face, through his hair, made a fist in front of his mouth and finished off the yawn.

'Its gonna take more than a few hours sleep

to get over that.' Lucy slammed shut the door, the two crossed the corridor and descended the stairs to the resonating sound of their shoes. At the bottom Malloy lunged for the handle of the door leading to the street, instead of opening it he paused, then turned to Lucy.

'Why've you not said anything about me kissing you the other night.'

Lucy smiled up at him.

'That was a kiss?' She rose onto tip toes, took his face in her hands, and pulled him easily toward her like he was a sapling tree bending to the strength of the wind. Her mouth opened and melted into his. She sucked lightly on his upper lip and her tongue playfully explored his mouth and met his. He stiffened against her, she felt a thrill of excitement and ran her hand down to his crotch.

'My, my, Officer Malloy, have we left our night stick in our pocket?'

'Get a damn room.' The rasp came from behind Lucy.

'Morning Mr Abelman.' Lucy recognised the voice, swung herself round one hundred and eighty degrees and at the same time opened the door, letting the old man out onto the street.

Mr Abelman glared at her as he passed.

'Randazzo, shoulda guessed, damn wops…like rabbits.'

'Love you too Mr Abelman.' Lucy said blowing him a kiss.

'Nem Zich a vaneh!' he strode away, flinging his arms around in annoyance.

Lucy stepped out onto the street and shouted after him, 'Rude old man, see you Saturday, usual time?'

Mr Abelman stopped at the cross walk, 'Yes, yes usual time, Saturday.'

Malloy joined Lucy on the sidewalk looking puzzled.

'He's teaching me to play Klaberjass.'

Malloy nodded none the wiser 'You're a surprising woman Sophia Lucia Radazzo, you wanna lift?'

'No, I'm good, thanks.' She pointed over her shoulder. 'Gotta…bus to catch,' she walked backward a few steps, waved briefly at Malloy, turned and set off down the road.

***

When Lucy arrived at work, she found it hard to concentrate, the image of the Zippo lighter on her kitchen table burned into her head. It called to her, impatient to be reunited with its other part, how she could achieve that, she had no idea.

She soon decided caffeine was the only way she'd get through the day, so went off to the staff room, and was opening a fresh jar of coffee when Chinah came in.

'You look miserable today.' Chinah noted.

'Thanks.' Lucy pursed her lips, picked up a spoon and used it to pierce the thin foil seal across the jar. She inhaled the fresh coffee aroma and felt instantly calmed.

'Shit, no comebacks?' Chinah leant against the wall and looked at Lucy in confusion.

'Not in the mood for you today, Chine.' Lucy took two coffee cups from the cupboard. 'Coffee?'

Chinah didn't answer, she simply glided swanlike over to her friend, her small legs shuffling beneath a skirt of fat.

'You seen something else in that mirror, that what it is?' She whispered.

Lucy looked around the room, three other employees were sat nearby, but they were too busy conversing excitedly about a recent night out together, to be bothered with what Chinah and Lucy were saying.

Lucy placed the coffee cups on the counter.

'You really think I'm gonna tell you after you

nearly lost me my job?'

'I've said sorry.' Chinah replied sheepishly. 'Besides you would hardly have lost your…'

'Seriously, you gonna start arguing with me?' Lucy interrupted.

Chinah sucked in her lips and placed her chubby index finger across them.

'You promise not to say anything?' Lucy folded her arms purposefully.

'Of course I do.' Chinah put on her most sincere of faces. 'I won't tell a soul.'

'Promise.' Lucy hissed under her breath.

'Yeeees…I…said…I…promise'.

Lucy returned to the coffee, put a large spoonful in each cup, poured in the boiling water and added a spot of milk to one, which she proffered to Chinah.

'Here, let's go to my office it's quieter.'

Chinah bristled with excitement, took the coffee from Lucy and followed her out into the corridor.

***

The only light came from the small torch he held between his teeth.

He laid her flat on the ground, eyes to the stars

and arranged her red dyed hair about her head. When he was satisfied with the scene, he ran his fingers over the staples and raw flesh where her lips had once been and instantly his mother's image came into his mind. He needed to be careful, he knew the fog of his childhood memories concealed blades. Tentatively he searched his mind for the good memory. A glimmer teased him, and he followed it. Several times darkness threaten to envelope it and drag it away to a place beyond retrieval, but he continued his pursuit and once it was found, he sheltered it carefully against the dark, and delighted in its glow.

It was, he remembered, the unfamiliar gentleness of the touch which wiped away the blood. Whose hands had those been and why did they soothe him when everywhere else there had been pain? Suddenly the memory started to shake itself free. He held on, but the darkness was too strong, and it tore at the glimmer until it faded back into the recesses of his mind. All that remained were memories of the evil words and pain which scratched and snicked at the structure of his young soul until a hole was torn, out of which drained all his humanity.

Close behind came the memory of being freed from his nightmarish life, only to find he and his mother sentenced to prison. She in Bedford Hills correctional facility and he in a society he knew nothing of.

He was bright enough to realise he had to be seen to fit in, he already knew how to control his emotions, he simply had to learn the correct answers to the litany of probing questions, keep quiet, do as he was told, show no anger or distress. In some ways things were no different to his previous life. It didn't take long for him to become invisible. Then as he grew into a teenager, things changed, he became aware of an attribute which was more helpful to him than anything he'd ever imagined. His mask, his veil of handsomeness, his beautiful face had become the most effective cloak to evil he could ever have wished to possess.

FOURTEEN

Calvin returned from lunch at Jakes 'Dogs 4 Dawgs' across from where he worked as a writer for the New York Wire. He stepped into the elevator and a stream of bodies followed filling the remaining area around him, bringing the small space alive with micro movements as everyone eased and arranged their bodies and bags into suitable positions. Calvin was as short as he was wide and some of the elevator's occupants took advantage of the available space above him by leaning over into the void. Little claustrophobic sweat beads popped from Calvin's forehead and he started to question his reasons for eating a third chilli dog at lunch as gas bubbled inside him with an undetermined destination. He briefly considered exiting and making his way to the cool quiet of the stairwell, but it was too late, the doors closed and the elevator began its ascent.

Mason Andrews, special news editor, a clear foot and a half taller and three times slimmer than Calvin, stood in the corner unnoticed by the many eyes focussed on the steel doors, until his low resonant voice singled him out.

'The article you ran last week about the woman with the mirror?'

Cal could only see Mason by twisting and tilting his head, like a chicken looking at the sky.

'I know it wasn't our usual type of article, but it filled a gap.' He replied defensively.

'Does it have legs though?' Mason turned slightly, inadvertently placing his groin against Calvin's elbow. 'Is there any more info from your friend?'

Calvin froze as Mason pressed against him, he tried subtly to disengage his arm by moving it back and forth, only to realise with horror that he was simply agitating Masons genitals. Thankfully the elevator pinged to a halt, a second later the doors sucked open, and its occupants flooded out into the corridor.

'No, but it's a crock anyway, are you sure about a follow up?' Calvin said panting, as he tried to match step with Mason, who was easily ploughing through the melee.

'A close personal friend of mine, Jim Carrera,'s

coming to town on tour with his Supernatural showcase. If we can run some stories like this… this mirror thing, it's gonna boost interest in his shows.' Mason came to a sudden stop, two women careered into his back, quickly apologised and flowed around him like he was a rock in a stream. 'In fact,' he said, taking his chin in his fist. 'Let's run a whole feature, see what you can come up with, ghost stories, ghouls, anything.'

Calvin saw his chance. 'I'm already on it, I've been told the mirror woman thinks she's gonna find our serial killer with it.'

Mason stared at Calvin, the crease between his brows deepened. 'The cops are gonna use a freakin' nut job to find the killer! Are you shitting me, and you wait til now to tell me this?' Mason was overjoyed. 'That's a damn story in itself, I've heard of using mediums before, but hell…Get me some copy, Q as P.' Mason continued down the corridor leaving Calvin standing.

'I don't think the cops are…I only spoke to my source this morning.' Calvin shouted redundantly.

Mason stopped at the door to his office. 'What are we calling this one again?'

'The article?' Calvin caught up to Mason.

'No, the serial killer?'

'Well remember I said, we'd decided, well, if

he's cutting off the lips of his victims, maybe he's a Stones fan, maybe he wants to find himself some Jagger lips'. Calvin added a laugh to soften the statement. 'So, we settled on The Jagger.'

Mason grinned and gave a little snort. 'Ah yes I remember, no, no I like it.' He disappeared into his corner office and the door closed automatically behind him.

As the excitement drained from Calvin's body, he realised he'd put himself in a difficult situation, the last time he'd spoken to Chinah, she'd made him promise not to divulge any more of what she'd told him, to anyone. He had to think of a way to get information from her, without her guessing what he was up to. This assignment might be his big break, he wasn't going to miss out on an opportunity to show Mason what he could do.

Calvin became aware of a hot dampness spreading from his armpits and immediately put his knuckles together in front of his chest and lifted his arms to let the air cool his sweat. He spotted a colleague leaning against the wall focusing on the contents of a binder.

'Hey Escher,' Calvin approached the man, flapping his elbows up and down like a chick testing its wings. 'You catch Game of Thrones last night'?

'Busy.' Escher mumbled without lifting his gaze from the page.

Calvin stretched out a hand and leant against the wall, Escher looked up briefly, 'No spoilers either, I hate it when you give the plot away'.

'Oookay, I'll catcha later.' Calvin took the hint and flapped his way to the vending machine to get a soda to help cool him down.

FIFTEEN

Lucy stood on the corner of Thayer and Nagel, waiting for Malloy, it was exactly 3pm. Behind her a billboard announced boldly.

> *AmerPhoenix Demolition.*
> *We raze. So you can rise.*

Beneath the words a male model wearing a hard hat and high visibility jacket posed, whilst behind him a shiny excavator, it's bucket inverted, threatened the remnants of a building.

Originally her client, a production company, booked a site through another agency, but at the last moment there were ground pollution issues and when the trainers of the dogs (which were integral to the plot) found out, they refused to let their valuable assets put a paw on the set. Maniac Locations came to the rescue. Lucy being a local, had knowledge of the imminent rezoning of certain areas of Inwood and quickly investigated several places including the storage facility and the adjoining derelict UPS distribution centre. The client was pleased with the locations and Lucy managed to negotiate a two-week window with the demolition and construction companies. So time was tight.

3.10pm, Lucy leant against the fence beneath the billboard, she took out her phone and scrolled quickly through the photographs she'd previously taken of the doors and windows of the UPS distribution centre and the storage facility. If her boss asked why she'd not been in the office that afternoon, the pictures would be her alibi. She looked up as a Buick station wagon approached and slowed to a stop. Its engine churned over like a shaken box of greasy nuts and bolts. She checked out the dents and scratched up paintwork, then looked to see what sort of person could possibly want to drive such a thing and saw Malloy at the wheel.

'What the hell!' She tried to put a lid on a laugh, but it spat out. The vehicles window rolled down. 'You expect me to get in that thing?'

'You're welcome to walk.' Malloy flung out his arm and motioned down the street.

'Well, I don't live too far away, I guess I could.' Lucy teased.

'It's a classic, get in.' Malloy reached over and popped open the door.

Lucy climbed in, only just managing to shut the door, before Malloy pulled out narrowly missing another car, which swerved and blared its horn.

'Jesus, I hope you drive your squad car better than this.'

A few minutes later they pulled up outside Lucy's apartment and were soon inside.

'Get some coffee going, I'll fetch the, the thing.' Lucy nodded her head toward the bathroom.

'How'd you like it?'

'Eh?'

'Coffee, how'd you like it?'

'Like my men, strong, no sugar.'

Five minutes later they sat at the table staring at the Mirror. Malloy picked up the Zippo lighter from the table and gave it to Lucy.

'Here goes.' He angled the mirror toward her.

Lucy shuffled in her seat to get comfy, sighed and began her questions.

'Show me who this belongs to.' She lifted the lighter so she could see its reflection in the glass.

The mirror misted and after a few seconds cleared, Lucy was disappointed to see nothing but the sight of her own image.

She turned to Malloy. Her reflection didn't.

Lucy jolted. 'Oh crap, I can't get used to this thing.' She held her chest and felt her heart race.

'I was just about to point out the lighter wasn't reflected, then you turned.' Malloy squeezed her shoulder reassuringly.

'Ok, so the lighter is mine now?' Lucy hadn't addressed the mirror, but it answered her anyway and showed her slightly shifted reflection once more.

'Try the cap.' Malloy leant across and prised off the top of the Zippo and handed it to Lucy.

'Ok.' Lucy held the lighter in one hand and the cap in the other. 'Where is the original cap like this?' She proffered the cap toward the glass. 'That goes on this lighter.' She assembled the two parts and twisted the lighter back and forth. The glass misted. Lucy looked at Malloy and realised they were holding their breath. The mirror seemed to be taking a while.

'It's like it's searching.' Malloy whispered.

'Maybe it's Googling.' Lucy replied, grinning.

The mist swirled and faded slightly. They continued to stare into the haze, Lucy chewed on her lip in nervous anticipation. The mist darkened again, the two looked at each other their brows crinkling in concert.

'Come on.' Lucy implored, returning her gaze to the mirror.

A little space at the bottom left of the mirror cleared to show the cap belonging to the Zippo.

A glance of surprise flashed between Lucy and Malloy.

The mist continued to disperse, revealing tassels like those of an old-fashioned couch, dirty and torn, then a shoe, no, a slipper, red, stained and bearing small brown circles of cigarette burn, then the leg of a table and a pile of magazines. On one, there was an address sticker.

'Bingo.' Malloy slammed his palm down on the table and stood quickly, the suddenness jerked the chair he sat on, sending it backward onto the floor with a bang.

Lucy began to stand to retrieve the chair, Malloy turned and bent to do the same. They both paused hands outstretched, temple to temple. Lucy turned to Malloy a millisecond later he turned to her. In a heartbeat, Lucy's lips covered his. They struggled to stand, staggering and reeling together until Lucy's back slammed against the wall, their mouths began to pounce between each other's necks, lips and cheeks, like starving hyenas on a carcass.

Lucy tore at the buttons on her cargo's, then unzipped Malloy's pants. He spun her round pulling down her panties at the same time. Lucy gasped as he pushed into her, she splayed her hands on the wall and shimmied her buttocks toward him. His hands shifted from the wall above her shoulders to her hips. He slammed into her forcefully, thrusted several more times, grunted through gritted teeth and withdrew. Lucy felt his hot liquid on her cool butt cheek. For several seconds the only movement was the expansion of their lungs. Malloy was the first to move, he stood back from Lucy and gently began to ease her panties back up her thighs. Lucy put her hands on his, to stop him, wiped her hand across her buttock and with her cargos still around her knees, shuffled over to the sink, flicking the white globules of fluid into the water before pulling her panties up the rest of the way.

She washed her hands before turning to Malloy and his lopsided grin.

'Well, I've not done that before.' He said tucking the last piece of shirt into his pants. 'I'm sorry it wasn't…you know, it's been a while.'

Lucy wandered over, tucked her hands around his buttocks and pulled him to her. 'What times your shift start?'

'Eight.'

Lucy looked at the clock.

'Ok, time for a bite to eat. Then it's my turn.' She patted his behind and went to the refrigerator. 'What you gonna do about, you know, the address…?' She opened the door and peered inside.

'I guess I'll check it out first, ask some questions, do some old detective work off the record, see if I can find some reason to go visit this guy.'

'What makes you think it's a guy?' Lucy moved aside some limp salad and pulled out a container of chopped chicken.

'It's always a guy.'

'Funny that's what Chinah said. You like chicken?' Lucy proffered the container.

'Chicken? Yeah, who doesn't. Who's Chinah?'

'Work colleague, friend.' Lucy shrugged one shoulder in a noncommittal way.

'Tell me again, what you do exactly?' Malloy lifted the chair from the floor, straddled it and folded his forearms across its back.

Lucy put the chicken on the side. 'I find places…' She took a pan from the drainer, doused it with olive oil and placed it on the burner.

'Like sets for the film industry,' she tipped the chicken pieces into the oil. 'Sometimes ad agencies, that sort of thing.' She went to the refrigerator and took out the salad.

'Anything I might've seen? He took a gulp of his coffee and grimaced.

'Cold already?' Lucy enquired. She passed by the cooker and flipped the pink chicken pieces until they were white side up.

'No, weird flavour.' Malloy said chewing the bad taste around his mouth.

Lucy placed the salad on the table, took the cup from him, sniffed and sipped a little.

'Shit I'm sorry, it mustn't have rinsed properly.' She poured the coffee down the sink along with hers. 'Soap, won't do you any harm, you'll be fine.' She picked up the salad from the table. 'Now where's the salad spinner.' Lucy said opening a cupboard door.

'It's in the dishwasher.' Malloy said nonchalantly.

Lucy looked at him puzzled. 'How d'y…'

Malloy turned the mirror toward her. It showed a salad spinner sitting amongst other items in a dishwasher.

'Thank God I didn't ask it where my virginity went.' As soon as the last word exited her mouth, Lucy pounced toward the mirror, too late, Malloy twisted it round to face him again.

'No, no, no.' She squealed, pulling at his fingers.

Malloy let go, Lucy fell back, hugging the mirror and laughing.

***

'So, what you got for me.' Mason stood over Calvin and stared at the computer screen.

'Well, I've padded out the mirror article, added this about a recent sighting of headless George Cooke at St. Pauls and this about the Well at 126th street. I sent Jerome down to interview one of the staff there who recently saw a…' Calvin looked up at Mason. 'Ghost'. He said with air quotes, before realising that Mason may actually believe in them, especially since he was a pal of Jim Carrera's. Calvin quickly resumed his pitch and hoped the visual sarcasm wouldn't affect Masons opinion of him. 'Escher's done an advertorial for Jim's show to run alongside the copy, looks pretty good too, he's gonna forward it to you.'

'Ok, good, good, I wanna get Jim's approval on all of this, his publicity agent's sending over some photographs to include.' Mason patted Calvin on the shoulder. 'I appreciate the extra work you're putting in for this, it won't go unnoticed.'

Calvin nodded politely, and inwardly hi-fived himself. Finally, he'd got some recognition for his work and all because of some crazy bitch who thought a mirror spoke to her.

***

He was not one for mysticism, superstition, or old wives' tales. He was a firm believer in the principal of Occam's razor, the least contestable conclusions are most likely to be correct. Ghosts were merely shadows. Black magic and voodoo used people's malleable minds upon themselves for curative or injurious purposes. And clairvoyants? Well, he thought they should be burned at the stake.

But what if this woman with the mirror knew something, actually knew something about him? What if, as with many charlatans, there was some knowledge behind her make-believe? He needed to find out. He looked at the name in the newspaper article and typed it into his computers' search engine.

A few seconds later he'd found her LinkedIn and Facebook profiles, including her work address. He searched through for any relevant information and discovered a picture of Chinah. He recognised her as his work colleagues on/off fuck buddy, she was the obvious source of Calvin's information. He scrolled further and found a picture of several women posed together in front of a bar, champagne glasses in their hands. Chinah and the woman were in the centre, heads together in a symmetrical droop of inebriation.

A Happy Birthday balloon floated above Chinah's head, and a caption read.

Friends and work colleagues for four years.

'Happy friendaversary, Lucy.' He took a shot of the screen with his phone, closed the window and deleted his search history.

SIXTEEN

'He's skinny, but he's good looking.' Chinah said widening her eyes and tilting her head at Lucy. 'I'll owe you one.'

Lucy shuffled items around her desk.

'Don't do that Puss in Boots thing, it may work on your boyfriend, but it doesn't work on me, you know I hate blind dates, they're always ugly pathetic specimens and I'm a sucker for a mercy fuck and I always regret it in the morning.' Lucy stapled several pieces of paper together at one corner and then continued to idly staple along one side.

'Afterwards, I can't get rid of them, they're all needy and whiney, they won't take the hint to get lost and I have to get nasty with them. I prefer good looking guys slightly outta my league, with them it's all about the sex, nothing more. That's suits me fine.'

Chinah fumbled around with her phone and showed Lucy a picture of two ugly men standing side by side in a grey office, one of them held a plaque with pride, the other pointed at the first guy with both his index fingers.

'This is my bae…' She pointed to the large man with the bald head. '…And that's his colleague receiving employee of the month.'

Lucy stared at the guy, he'd got a face like a pug dog and the stature to match. Chinah scissored her fingers across the screen to enlarge the background.

'And here, at the back, is your date.' She stared at Lucy triumphantly and waited for a response.

The guy in question was facing but not actually looking at the camera and probably had no idea he was part of the photograph. He was bent around a computer, a USB cable in one hand, plug in the other. He was incredibly handsome, but in a boring symmetrically featured way. He wore a tight Tee and skinny pants. So, it was easy to see the outline of his body, which was tightly muscled and sinewy like a long-distance runner.

'Deal.' Lucy flashed a grin at Chinah.

'Thats great.' Chinah exclaimed, clicking the home button on her cell. 'I'm hoping a double date will make Cal take the next step and get serious about our relationship. I only ever get to see him at my place and we just…' Chinah smiled salaciously. 'Well, you know…and that's it, that's all we ever do.' She flung her phone back into her purse. 'A guys gotta commit sometime Lucy.'

'Yeah, but most guys just wanna commit adultery or bigamy…or suicide, committing to a relationship is the last thing they wanna do.' Lucy thought of Malloy and Tom. Maybe she was being harsh.

'Look who's talking.' Chinah's voice raised an octave. 'I ain't never known a woman so scared to be with someone.'

'Scared, what makes you think I'm scared? I just don't want the…hassle.' Lucy moved her mouse to take the computer out of sleep mode.

'That stuck in your throat didn't it? I don't think you realise why you do what you do.' Chinah walked over to the door. Lucy ignored her and set about typing an email.

'Your dad abandoned you, your mum abandoned you…'

'They didn't abandon me, they died.' Lucy said flatly.

'Same thing to a child.' Chinah pulled at the door handle. 'Times a ticking, Sofia Lucia Randazzo, no one's gonna save you 'sept yourself.'

SEVENTEEN

There was boarding over the window of the old bookstore, clearly it had been unoccupied for a long time. To the side there was a small paint peeled door, a stubby screwdriver protruded from the space where the handle had once been, Malloy twisted it and pushed, for a second nothing happened then the door gave way, only a little, but enough to see a pile of debris behind it. Shoving hard with his shoulder and foot simultaneously, Malloy made a gap large enough to squeeze through.

'Police officer!' He waded through the mail and junk food containers which littered the hall, as he moved toward the stairs his nose caught the pungent tendrils of death, each step the smell grew stronger, on the second floor he felt bile rising in his throat as the smell became almost unbearable. A door was open, the first in a row of three. Malloy shouted his presence once more, still no one replied. He sidled along the wall and peered round the door jamb. The sight of the body was no surprise to Malloy, he'd seen enough in his time, many worse than this, he could tell by the decomposition, the woman had been dead maybe four or five weeks. She wore a short pink skirt and a blue Tee, which was gathered up under her armpits to reveal her horribly bloated body. Dark green and purple blotches merged on the surface of her skin like some macabre camouflage. One leg sagged over the edge of the couch, the skin on the inner thigh, fragile with disintegration had torn slightly, causing a brown viscous liquid to ooze out.

A little hot acid pumped into Malloy's mouth, he turned his head, spat it out and stepped toward the body, hand over his nose and mouth.

Remembering what the mirror had shown, he moved his foot through the tassels along the underside of the couch edge and touched something light, he swept past again and hooked it out. It was the top of a Zippo lighter. The mirror was right. He jerked his head toward the coffee table, his blood chilled when he saw the magazine, just as it was in the mirror. He leant over, moved the top copy which partially covered the address sticker on the edition beneath and read the scrawl above the street name, Jaqueline Falconi.

As Malloy straightened up, his knee accidentally touched the woman's leg, the thigh tear gave way a little more, sending a fresh wave of stench into the air, Malloy decided he'd seen enough and ran out onto the street making sure he left the door wide open so he could claim probable cause for entry, he took several large breaths of unadulterated city air, then called in the incident.

EIGHTEEN

There were only four other people eating in the garlic infused pizza restaurant, which for a Friday night worried Lucy somewhat.

'There's not many here.' She whispered to Chinah as they were shown their seats by a diminutive pigtailed waitress. 'I'm not gonna get sick, am I?'

'It's not long opened, not many know about it.' Chinah took the large white square of napkin from her plate, unfolded it and tucked it in her neck. Then she reached over and took one from the next place setting, shook it out and placed it across her lap. 'They put their first ad in Cals paper, last week, he's got coupons.' She picked up the menu and began to read the items out loud.

'Prosciutto and mozzarella, Focaccia, Insalata, Yeah, I don't think, Tonno E Ceci, what the hells…'

She flipped the menu over and drew a crooked finger down the line of specials.

The door to the restaurant opened and the fat guy from the picture Chinah had shown Lucy entered. The pigtailed waitress tucked an errant corner of her shirt into her waistband and approached him. He waved her away and pointed to Lucy and Chinah's table.

The waitress nodded and relaxed back onto one of the fake pantheonic pillars.

'Ladies, apologies for being late.' Calvin's voice boomed before him. Chinah sprang from her chair and launched herself towards him, Calvin braced himself.

'Bae, you made it.' Chinah threw her arms around Calvin's neck, and he disappeared from Lucy's sight. Several seconds later the top of his red face popped out over Chinah's shoulder.

'You must be Lucy.' He said, pulling himself from Chinah's grasp. Lucy half expected to hear a pop as if a squid and octopus had been forcibly separated. Calvin held his arms out to Lucy, she stood quickly to avoid an embarrassing face to stomach hug, grabbed his fore arms, to preserve a distance between them and deftly placed a kiss on his cheek.

'Great to meet you.' She said as convincingly

as she could and immediately sat.

'And you! Chinah's told me all about you, my colleague is really psyched, should be here any moment'. He pulled out a chair equidistant from both Lucy and Chinah, swiped away some invisible piece of detritus from the seat, and sat.

'Funny.' Lucy said picking up the menu. 'Chinah's told me absolutely nothing about you.'

'Lucy!' Chinah placed the menu down on the table and gave Lucy an indignant stare. 'I so have!'

Lucy pulled a comic face like she was thinking hard.

'No, can't think of anything, except about the fu…'

'What's everyone eating?' Chinah blurted.

Calvin seemed totally oblivious to the train of conversation and peered at the menu.

'Maybe we should wait for Escher.' He finished with a rising inflection.

Chinah looked at her phone. 'He's already twenty minutes late, let's order.' Not waiting for an answer, she waved over the waitress and ordered. Lucy and Calvin followed suit.

'Well then where did you two lovebirds meet?' Lucy rested her chin on her knuckles.

'I wouldn't say we're exac…' Calvin began. Chinah halted him with a hand on his forearm and claimed the conversation.

'Well, I got this free gym session offer.' Chinah bubbled, eyes like two polished pearls. 'And decided I could maybe do with losing a few pounds.' She shifted uneasily in her seat.

Lucy denied a smirk which threatened her lips.

'Anyway, I saw Calvin.' She threw him a honeyed smile, to which Calvin did not reciprocate. 'And thought he looked delicious.' She patted his forearm.

'So, he was like, on the treadmill, he kept looking at me and smilin' so I go up to him and say…I can help you burn some calories baby, which don't involve this kinda equipment.' She laughed raucously at her own joke. 'N,' you know what he did?' She stroked down the side of Calvin's cheek and held his chin momentarily.

'No, what?'

'He slid straight off that machine and landed at my feet!'

The waitress appeared, a plate in either hand and another balanced along her forearm. Conversation stopped as she deftly delivered each meal. It didn't go unnoticed by Lucy that Calvin's eyes slipped salaciously over every inch of the waitress's figure.

Not overly particular about type then. Lucy

thought.

'So, I said to him…' Chinah continued. 'I'll take that as a yes then.' She turned to Calvin and screwed up her nose.

'We've not been back to the gym since have we sweet cheeks?' She slid her hand under the table and squeezed Calvin's thigh hard enough to cause him to flinch.

NINETEEN

It was back in the summer of 2017, when Autumn left her home in Worcester Massachusetts and took the greyhound to New York. To find fame and fortune on Broadway just as her sister Rain had.

But for Autumn things didn't pan out so well, she wasn't as pretty, intelligent or talented as Rain and whilst she waited for her dream audition, she worked in a diner as did many hundreds of others awaiting their big break. It was still a tightly held belief (albeit a myth conjured by the golden era of Hollywood) that acting hopefuls could be picked from obscurity whilst serving tables and subsequently catapulted to stardom.

It was whilst working at the Chantilly diner that she met Move, Anthony Movelli, busboy and general dog's body. Move introduced her to Crystalmeth and they fell in love. But as the saying goes, twos company and three's a crowd and soon after that first encounter Move was sidelined.

A little less than four months after Autumn arrived in New York, she found herself on her knees in the back of Franks car lot, trying not to throw up as she took a stranger's penis into her mouth for the first time. With the cash, she bought a half gram of Ice, to stop the grouch gremlins digging in her brain.

Too quickly, the use of her body in exchange for cash became the norm, she found it an effective way to keep her habit going, even when she discovered she was pregnant. Too late to abort, she let the baby grow inside her. Numbed by the Ice, she found it easy to deny the child's existence Months later the frail girl was born by emergency caesarean. Autumn held her briefly, before handing the pale bundle to its new parents, only then did she wonder what damage her addiction may have done.

When Autumn finally returned to the derelict house where she'd lived with several other meth heads, it was boarded up and everyone had moved on.

She had no choice but to go to Pearl.

Pearl was bottom girl for Antwon, three years she'd ran the track for him. Whenever he was away or incapacitated, it was she who took the money, ran interference, recruited new girls and dealt with any problems.

She took Autumn under her wing, cleaned her up and looked after her whilst her scar healed and when Autumn was ready, Pearl assigned her a spot on Starr Street, near the corner of Cypress avenue. She anticipated Autumn's long auburn hair and innocent face would make Antwon good money.

She was right, within minutes of Autumn being out, an old grey Toyota screeched to a stop, its driver signalled to her. She leant in, the John stared straight ahead, his face mottled orangish red by the light of the gauges on the dash.

'Get in.'

Autumn took a quick scope round, nodded briefly to Pearl, then slid into the seat beside the John. She slammed shut the car door as they pulled into the flow of traffic.

'Take a left here.' Autumn gestured to a side street.

The John continued past the turn.

'I've got somewhere, I'll pay double for your time.'

A small flux of anxiety-fuelled adrenaline shot around Autumn's body. Even so, she quickly convinced herself everything would be ok; besides she needed every dime, there was a long list of expenses she'd incurred whilst Pearl got her clean.

The John shoved several twenties between her thighs.

'Consider that a down payment.'

Autumn tucked the cash into her bra.

Several minutes later they pulled up outside a disused bookstore. The John got out, went round to Autumns side, opened the car door and held out his hand for her.

Autumn looked at his open palm, soft hands, moisturised. Not her usual John.

'I'm good.' She said refusing his offer of help, 'I'm a sure thing, this ain't no date.'

She followed him across the sidewalk to a kick-worn door and watched as he took a stubby screwdriver from his pocket, jammed it into the hole where the door handle had once been, and twisted. There was a click. The John leant his shoulder against the door and laboured to push it open, a piece of wooden trim got stuck beneath and grated against the cement. Autumn grit her teeth and shivered at the unsettling sound, the John squeezed through and signalled Autumn to follow.

The entrance hall was small and smelled of mushrooms and damp cardboard. They made their way through cans, pizza boxes and other junk to the stairway. It was obvious to Autumn that no-one had lived there for a long while.

'This your place?' She quizzed, as she passed quills of nicotine-stained wallpaper hanging from the drywall.

'It belongs to a friend.'

A bead of nervous sweat tickled a random trail between Autumns breasts. She scrubbed the heel of her hand against her Tee to halt its descent.

At the top of the stairs a door opened onto a tiny living room, the centre of which was taken up with an old rust red couch. Next to it was a small table piled high with magazines and in the corner a tv with an old-fashioned curved screen. A crocheted throw on the back of the couch hinted at there once having been an elderly occupant.

Autumn felt the tug of the Johns grip on her wrist and realised she was holding her ground in the doorway. He pulled her round to face him and walked her backward to the couch.

'You sure do remind me of my mother' He studied her face, reached out and touched her hair.

'Whatever gets you off baby, times running on.'

He grabbed her by the shoulder, the fabric of her tee tore a little as he pulled her to his steely face. 'I told you I'd pay for your time.'

He pushed her backward, she felt the touch of fabric on the back of her calves and the tassels of the couch skirt on her ankles. The John reached into his pocket and counted out a hundred dollars.

'Now shut it.' He said slamming the cash on the table next to some magazines.

Autumn sat down, pulled up her skirt and slid her butt until it hung halfway over the edge of the couch.

'Is this how you want it?' She opened her legs.

The John contemplated the pink frills of her pussy and then caught sight of the scar across her belly.

'You got a kid?' He cocked his head to one side.

'No, not anymore I ain't, what's it to you.'

He reached into his jeans and pulled out a zippo lighter, tint embossed with a camel's face. Autumn shifted uneasily on the couch. From his shirt pocket the John took a pack of Lucky Strikes, placed one in his mouth, flicked open the lighter and lit the cigarette.

Autumn drew her buttocks back onto the seat and looked at the money out the corner of her eye. The John sucked the smoke into his mouth and inflated his lungs to their capacity to obtain the full effects of the nicotine.

'So, where's the kid now?'

Autumn shrugged her shoulders. 'I dunno, what the fuck's it to you, anyhow?'

The John stared down at her, took another long draw, blew out the smoke and then rested the cigarette between his lips, the smoke made him squint as it trailed up past his right eye.

'I ain't got time for this bullshit.' Autumn's words slapped the quiet air, like someone shouting 'fuck' during a church service. She grabbed the notes from the table. 'Money for my time.' She snarled, and attempted to bolt past the John, but he grabbed her.

'Why'd you do it.' his palm slammed into her chest and sent her flying back onto the couch.

'Why didn't you love your baby?' He screwed the cigarette into his fist, ignoring the burn.

'What?' Autumn gasped.

'I said why didn't you love your baby?'

'Look.' Autumn reached her hand toward him defensively and tried a disarming smile. 'I'm sorry if…'

'You're *sorry*?' With a pained look on his face, he shoved the bent stub into his pocket along with the lighter. Autumn instantly knew why he'd not thrown it to the floor, she stood to make her escape, but he was quicker.

He grabbed her throat with his right hand and punched her in the side with his left fist, the impetus caused them both to topple back onto the couch, dust plumed into the air. His left hand joined his right around her throat. She tried to pull his hands away, but he was incredibly strong for such a wiry man.

As she tried to disengage his fingers, he lifted his torso away from her, grabbed her hands and in one delicate gymnastic move pounced his knees onto her arms pinning them down as he sat across her chest. He returned his hands to her throat. She tried to scream but there was no breath to pass over her vocal cords. Her arteries strained against the pressure of his grip. Autumn flailed twisting her legs and hips violently to throw him off, a vertebra popped in her lower back and the pain seared through her. The Johns hands tightened on her throat, Autumn's heart fell out of beat and her head began to swim.

I can't die, no, no, someone help me!

A last wave of adrenaline crashed through her, followed by calm. Sadness visited for a second and then…nothing.

The John released his grip and stood. As he did

so, the little silver lid from his cigarette lighter, broken off during the attack, dropped unnoticed to the floor. It knocked silently against the Johns shoe and disappeared behind the couch tassels. He adjusted his shirt, tucked it into his pants, sniffed, then gagged. The girl's bowels and bladder had released, something he'd not anticipated. He looked at her face, red with petechia. There was no horror in him, no remorse, only a feeling of calm.

TWENTY

Chinah looked at her phone, 9.40 pm still no sign of Escher. She was starting to feel embarrassed and slightly annoyed. Tonight, was meant to create a stronger bond between her and Calvin, mutual friends meant more nights out and the opportunity to deepen their relationship.

She was twenty-seven and never been engaged, time to change up a gear and push for what she really wanted. If she were going to get married before her thirtieth birthday, she needed to turn the pressure on, gently, gradually and without diversion.

'That's what he said, honest to God.' Lucy took a swig of her beer and banged the bottle on the table.

Chinah had daydreamed through the conversation and had no idea why Calvin flung back his head and barked a laugh.

'Lucy, you're hilarious.' Calvin burped loudly causing a fresh bout of laughter.

Chinah looked from Lucy to Calvin, eyes narrow with concern. She tried to formulate something witty to say to swing the conversation back to her, when she felt a presence and noticed both Calvin and Lucy looking just beyond her. Chinah turned and saw it was Escher.

'At last.' She sighed.

'Buddy, take a seat.' Calvin, leant forward and gestured to the space next to Lucy.

Escher passed Calvin and the two grabbed each other's wrists in a brief manly shake.

Lucy took the opportunity to have a good look at her date. He wore a deep blue suit with matching waistcoat, a pair of dark tinted sunglasses pushed high on the bridge of his nose and on his wrist, he sported an Omega Seamaster. It looked like a real one, but Lucy wasn't sure, she glanced down at his shoes. She'd heard somewhere, you can tell a person's true worth from the shoes they wore. Escher's were expensively made, she didn't know by whom, but she could tell they were quality.

'Tom Ford.' Escher lifted his right foot and moved it from side to side, showcasing his high shine Derby shoes.

'I forgot to tell you.' Calvin interjected. 'Escher's a self-made man, made an obscene heap of money from property, only works for the paper a couple o' days a week, to keep him outta trouble.'

'Well hell,' Lucy blurted…'take a seat rich boy.'

Escher sat, an enthusiastic waitress bustled over and took his order. As the four of them waited for their food, Calvin told a rather boring story about a works Christmas party which both he and Chinah had attended, thankfully the food arrived quickly, and the conversation turned to a different topic.

'I had an aunt, she was part Italian, she used to make the most incredible spaghetti carbonara, so creamy.' Calvin twisted his fork against his spoon and tried to cram the pasta into his mouth before it unravelled, he almost managed it, except for one slippery plump strand which snaked momentarily from his mouth before being sucked back in, it's retreat left white globs of sauce on his chin, he licked as far as he could and then wiped the rest away with his napkin. Lucy noticed he looked longer than was necessary at the fabric, she figured in other company he would have sucked the drops from it.

'Sushi.' Escher didn't look up from his food

but continued to slice his meatballs in half one by one. 'You gotta admire the precision.'

'I'm all about the taste.' Chinah interjected. 'If it's chunky and salty, Mmm Mmm I'm putting that in my mouth.' She smirked and winked at Lucy.

'Don't.' Calvin said flatly, 'This is not the place.'

'Don't! Don't! You ain't telling me what I can and can't say, if this…' Chinah wagged her index finger back and forth between them. '…is gonna progress, you need to know…'

'What's this…?' Calvin imitated Chinah's gesture.

Chinah frowned. 'Our relationship silly.' She rolled her eyes and glanced toward Lucy with a sigh.

'He's already engaged.' Escher mumbled, forking a piece of meatball and placing it in his mouth.

'He's what?' Chinah glared at Escher who continued to eat his meatballs seemingly unaware of the shit storm he'd begun. Chinah lifted her substantial rear end from her seat and turned her attention to Calvin. 'You're what!'

'Well, I, we never…' Calvin tried quickly to find the right words to ameliorate the situation.

'Blah blah blah, meh meh meh.' Chinah pushed Calvins plate of spaghetti carbonara into his shirt, then after calmly wrapping her garlic breads in a napkin swaggered out onto the street, nose in the air.

'Okay.' Lucy said watching through the window as Chinah hailed a cab. 'My place for drinks?'

Escher immediately laid down his fork, walked round the table, took a heap of twenties from his jacket pocket and thrust them into Calvin's hand. 'On me.' He patted Calvin's shoulder a couple of times. 'See you at the office.'

Calvin looked at the cash and nodded, stunned for a second or two at the suddenness of everyone leaving. He looked up and caught the eye of the waitress. 'Large scotch, no ice.'

Lucy was already out the door, she passed the restaurant window and glanced in at Calvin, he was calmly waiting for the mess of spaghetti to fall onto the plate he held in his lap. When it landed, he passed the plate to the waitress in exchange for the scotch, which he threw down his throat in one.

'Lucy!'

She turned; Escher was holding the door to a cab.

'Don't worry about him'. He said, signalling Lucy to get in. 'He's an asshole.'

TWENTY-ONE

Lucy broke open the bottle of fifteen-year-old single malt whiskey, a gift from one of her clients and poured herself and Escher a large drink. For a while they chatted about what happened between Chinah and Calvin in the restaurant, then out of the blue Escher suggested a game of cards, which at first Lucy thought strange, until he announced the game he had in mind was strip poker. Lucy, already pretty drunk, needed no persuading. As they played, she came to realise, either Escher was very good at cards, or he was an accomplished cheat. The game ended after less than twenty minutes, with Lucy completely naked and Escher having lost nothing but a shoe.

'I guess I win.' He said as he watched Lucy throw her panties on top of her discarded clothes and walk toward the door. 'Wait come back here.'

Lucy returned to the table, Escher stood, put down his glass. walked behind her, took off his tie, and deftly bound her wrists. Lucy felt his breath on her back and was immediately aroused.

'Sit down.'

Lucy obeyed. He moved in-front of her, parted her legs and slid his hand between her thighs, Lucy closed her eyes and moaned as he entered her with his fingers. She pressed her feet into the floor, lifted her buttocks slightly and began to oppose the rhythm of his hand.

She gasped out a little 'no.' when he suddenly stopped, he ignored her, wrapped his arms around her hips and pulled her to the edge of the seat. Moments later his mouth was on her, sucking and licking. Lucy needed to have him, to feel him inside her, she tried to free her wrists to touch him, but the binds were too tight.

'Close your eyes.' He splayed his index and middle finger and ran them down the front of Lucy's eyelids, she thought it a slightly creepy thing to do, but she obliged and closed them. He slipped his hands under her thighs, linked his fingers beneath her, lifted her from the chair and carried her to the bedroom like she was nothing more than a towel thrown over his shoulder.

'Eyes closed, don't move.' His voice was quiet

yet commanding as he laid her on the bed.

Lucy heard him leave the room, she laid still until he returned a few minutes later. There was a clink as something glass was placed on the nightstand and then the pull of the mattress as Escher sat next to her on the bed. Something ice cold and wet touched her thigh and she twitched.

'Keep still.' He ordered.

Lucy's chest heaved in anticipatory breaths. The ice cube started its way up the inside of her leg, its chill tingle reached the top of her thigh and turned inward toward her close shaven hair, stopping momentarily at her vulva. Lucy arched her back, her eyes still closed, as Escher pushed the cube between her lips and circled it round her clitoris and back down, to below her wet opening, again he paused, this time to pinch lucy's nipple hard causing her to let out a sound of pain.

'Shh, quiet baby.' He said and pushed the ice cube into her, then pulling her to the edge of the bed he knelt and began to bring her to orgasm with his fingers and tongue.

'Fuuuuuuuuck.' The word came out harsh and animalistic, as finally Lucy's whole body crashed into a hot sea of intense sensation, her heart banged against the inside of her chest, perspiration coalesced into beads of sweat, which trickled down her forehead and cleavage.

She opened her eyes and a little laugh escaped her as she realised Escher was still fully dressed. She wiped her clammy palms on the bed cover and began to sit up. Escher placed his hand onto her chest.

'Lay still.'

Carefully he folded the top blanket around her until she resembled an Egyptian Mummy. Lucy wondered, as she tried to gain control of her breathing, what reciprocal sexual act she'd be asked to perform. Then as if he'd heard her thoughts, Escher began to take off his clothes, he folded each item neatly and placed them one by one on top of the other, eventually he stood before her in navy socks and white boxers. To Lucy's surprise, instead of laying with her on the bed, he lifted the covers, shuffled himself down into the sheets and closed his eyes.

'Goodnight, Lucy Randazzo.'

Lucy didn't reply, she stared at him curiously. Regardless of her having achieved orgasm she still wanted full contact sex, it just felt wrong not to after what they'd done, you don't lick a popsicle then put it back in the freezer. Wriggling her arm out of the blanket, Lucy felt under the mattress, for a condom, she kept them just in case, as some guys, not many, but some, didn't seem to trust her when she said she was protected or when she said she got regular checks at the clinic. She put the condom between her teeth, unwrapped herself and attempted to climb under the sheets next to Escher, he instantly rolled away, tucking a section of sheet beneath him before rolling back onto it to create a barrier between them. She took the hint, covered herself back up with the blanket and was soon asleep.

At 3am Lucy woke with a dry mouth and a full bladder. She watched Escher's eyelids for a few seconds to make sure he was definitely sleeping before she crept out of bed. As she tip-toed to the door she pushed an errant strand of hair from her face and remembered all she'd divulged to Escher during their alcohol fuelled card game only hours before. She'd ranted on about the mirror, its powers, what happened with the boy, plus she'd exaggerated about how she was helping the police with their murder investigations. He'd been polite, not laughed or called her crazy. But then in Lucy's experience, guys would agree the world was flat if they thought it would get them laid.

She slipped out of the darkened room along the hall into the bathroom and sat crookedly on the toilet seat, aiming her stream to the side of the bowl to make as little noise as possible. Her head felt hollow and weary from the alcohol. She finished peeing, wiped herself, washed and dried her hands and was about to leave the bathroom, when she caught sight of the mirror on the shelf. The cool moonlight from the window cast a hazy Lalique shimmer across its surface and Lucy noticed something that hadn't been there last time she'd looked, a thumb print on the glass. Her curiosity aroused, she pressed her thumb on the clean spot directly above and noted the print she'd made was smaller.

Checked it out then did ya, Escher Balodis?

Lucy felt a stir of unease, there was something off kilter about him, something she'd not come across previously, it wasn't the sex thing, she'd done all kinds of kinky stuff before. It was something deeper than that, though she couldn't put her finger on it. She took her dressing gown from the hook on the door and decided to spend the rest of the night on the couch.

TWENTY-TWO

The following morning Lucy was woken by a creak in the hall. She presumed Escher was leaving, so kept her eyes closed and hoped that if he looked in, he'd see she was asleep and go on his way, no pressure for him to interact. *Au revoir Mr Balodis.*

They wouldn't have to say the usual awkward goodbyes, both parties knowing they'd no intention of seeing each other again yet pretending they would.

'I've made pancakes.' Escher whispered through the gap in the door.

Fuck! Lucy braced herself, held her breath and thought about how best to answer. 'That's thoughtful of you.' She managed to muster a breezy tone as she wondered where the hell in her kitchen, he'd found ingredients to make pancakes. She listened to his footsteps fade as he returned to the kitchen, then stretched, yawned, and stood slowly, stiff from the awkward position she'd slept in. Alert in case of Escher's return, she quickly poked her fingers under her arm pits and between her legs and took a sniff.

Bearable.

She re-tied her dressing gown belt with a double knot and went through to the kitchen. The aroma of coffee swathed her like a warm blanket in damp earthy woods. Escher sat at her table, he looked impeccable, his white shirt showed hardly a crease. A small unfamiliar cut-glass vase, set in the centre of the table sparkled with fresh water. Several stems of cheery yellow chrysanthemum daisies poked out from amongst green maple-shaped leaves.

He placed a plate of pancakes in front of Lucy, each one had been folded, cut in half and arranged fan-like across the plate. Over the top a shiny red sauce slowly lost its helical shape as it settled. A sliced strawberry its leaves intact, decorated the edge.

'You've been...busy.' Lucy pulled out a chair, sat down crossed legged and tucked the bottom corners of her dressing gown into her lap.

'I went for a morning stroll...picked up a few things.' He proffered a fork to Lucy.

'Thanks.' She took it and made a stab at the pancakes.

Ok, so you're gonna take a bit more effort than usual to get rid of.

She looked up at Escher, he was pouring coffee into two large cups.

I'd never have guessed you were this type of guy, and I'm rarely wrong.

'What do you think?' Escher nodded to her plate.

Lucy swallowed.

'Fantastic, your mum teach you to cook?'

Escher's eyes hardened and his whole body visibly stiffened, for the briefest of moments, a bat black look flew across his face, enough for Lucy to realise she'd picked at a scab, a canker, which was best left alone. Her previous hunch was correct, she could trust her instincts, this fantasy of a breakfast had simply blindsided her.

'I took classes.' Escher's face softened slightly. 'Long time ago.' He picked up his coffee and blew the steam from its surface.

Lucy realised this handsome bachelor hadn't been overlooked in this ant's hill of a city. This guy was flawed and not in the usual way, not in the, I've been hurt by a recent bad relationship, kinda way. But more like…I've got some crazy shit in my closet and a collection of cat skulls in a trunk under my bed kinda way. She'd have to be careful about how she brought this flirtation to an end.

'This is all very lo…'

'That mirror…' he stopped Lucy short. 'The one you told me about last night, the one you found the boy with, hows it work, can anyone use it?'

Lucy was right; Escher had looked at it.

'Well, as I said, the police found the boy, not the mirror.'

'But it can find things, you're not denying that?'

Lucy didn't feel comfortable with the way he said 'denying' as if she were on trial or something.

'I shouldn't have said anything, it's silly, I was drunk, do you really think a mirror can find things?' She gave an unconvincing laugh. Escher's expression was blank as he walked to her side and grabbed her arm just above the elbow.

'Let's go and see.' His grip tightened.

Lucy was momentarily shaken.

I'm alone, the guy next door's out at this time of day, shift work, so no use screaming, but then Escher's not gonna rape me, if last night's anything to go by, chill see what he wants…

'Humor me,' Escher pulled on her arm and Lucy immediately released the fork.

She rose slowly, her eyes searched the room

for a weapon, as she contemplated what to do in case something nuts happened. She allowed him to lead her through the hall to the bathroom. Once there Escher let go of her arm, put his hand in the small of her back and gently but firmly pushed her inside, he stood in the doorway, arms behind his back like a soldier.

Lucy turned to him and pasted a disarming smile across her lips.

'C'mon, this is silly.'

Escher stepped in, picked up the mirror and faced it toward Lucy.

'Ask it to find my waistcoat.' Escher raised the mirror slightly.

'But I…'

'Do it!' His temper flared and then blew out as quick as a match in a storm. 'I'm sorry, please… please say the words.'

Lucy chewed her lip, she couldn't think of a way out of the situation, her mind swirled with too many, 'What ifs', impossible to consolidate into any concrete plan of action.

Escher scared her, there was no doubt of that.

'Ok.' She stared at her pale reflection and said flatly. 'Where's…Escher's…waistcoat?'

Escher held the mirror by its stem and moved it away, so both he and Lucy could see the smokiness creep across their images in the glass. Escher's knuckles grew white as he squeezed the neck of the mirror. His excitement was tangible.

A gauzy vision appeared amongst the smokiness and began to form a picture. At first it revealed a nacre button, then a section of Escher's waistcoat. Adjacent to it was a lilac and green floral printed fabric. Lucy recognised the pattern as belonging to a dress she'd bought several summers ago, which hung unworn at the far end of her wardrobe, waiting for the right event and the right amount of sunshine.

Lucy felt sick, she'd revealed too much to a guy who was nothing more than a one-night stand, an unknown quantity. Look what happened when she'd told Chinah, about the mirror, a supposed friend, the story had been skewed and splashed across a quarter page of the New York Wire and on top of that, her job had been threatened. God knows what would happen now a stranger had seen the mirror's capabilities. She imagined herself tied to a stake surrounded by her friends and colleagues each brandishing a stick of kindling with which to stoke the pyre that burned at her feet. The ritual burning of the witch.

One thing she knew, he was not afraid, not like she or Malloy had been. Escher was engrossed, he turned the mirror around and around in his hands, as fascinated as if he'd discovered Aladdin's lamp in the Cave of Wonders.

Escher's reflected grin widened, his stomach knotted with excitement, with this mirror he would make his wish come true, all those private detectives he'd hired had been useless, at last with this mirror and Lucy, he could find her.

Twenty-Three

'You went home with him didn't you, you dirty whore.' Chinah said sticking her head through the door of Lucy's office.

Lucy looked up momentarily from her computer, then turned her attention back to the monitor and continued scrolling.

'I said…'

'I heard what you said Chinah, and I'm choosing to ignore you.'

'Oh,' Chinah slumped against the door frame and scowled at Lucy. 'No minute by minute, finger by dick breakdown of your sordid night then? What's up, didn't nothing happen?'

'I don't feel like it this morning.'

'Ha, ha, is that what he said, he couldn't get morning wood, so Lucy's upset.' Chinah walked over and stroked Lucy's hair like she was a puppy. 'Poor baby.'

'He's a dick.' Lucy said slapping Chinah's hand away.

'I thought that was the whole point, you like dick.'

'Yes, no, that guy's a genuine dick.' Lucy swivelled in her chair to face Chinah. 'Don't ever set me up again.'

'Aw LuLu, the number of guys you get through, there's bound to be a catfish or two.'

'Catfish, I don't mind, it's tarantulas I'm avoiding, there's something not right about him Chinah, something unnerving'.

'There it is, the excuse'.

Lucy's phone rang and she gestured to Chinah to leave the room.

'Yello.'

'You still meeting for girls' night?' Chinah interrupted.

Lucy gave a staccato nod, Chinah jiggled her fingers in a wave and disappeared out the door.

'We've had a development.' Malloys voice sounded strained.

'Hello Lucy, how you doin?'

'Oh, yeah, yeah sorry, you ok?' He didn't wait for an answer. 'Listen, there's no time to talk.'

'Ok, forget it.' Lucy said with an exaggerated sigh. 'Go ahead, what development?'

'I went to the address.' Malloy placed the words carefully, as if he were laying bricks.

'What address?'

'The one…' there was a short silence, then he continued in a quieter voice. 'In the mirror.'

'Oh, wow, and?'

'There was a body, a woman, don't know who, but it wasn't the tenant. Peroni, Maroni or something…Falconi, that was her name, Jaqueline Falconi, no she's alive and living with her daughter in Montreal. She, the dead woman was a red head, a real red head, by the state of decomposition, this could be our guys first victim and…I found the lid, the Zippo lid, underneath the sofa.'

'So, it works, the mirror, it really, really works, not just things we've hidden, but…' Lucy's excitement was audible.

'Lucy, you can't tell anyone…'

'But I…'

'Anyone, Lucy, if this gets out…'

Lucy thought about what had happened with Escher and decided not to tell Malloy. It was up to her to deal with the fallout from last night, besides it didn't seem right to tell him the reason why Escher had been in her apartment all evening.

'Ok, I'll stay shtum.' She didn't cross her fingers, as her sentence was in the future tense, and therefore couldn't be considered a lie.

'Good, I'll keep you updated…'

For a few seconds Lucy listened to dead air.

'Malloy? You there?'

'Yeah, I was just thinking, that mirror, why does it do it, what's its secret, where's it come from, I mean before your great aunt had it?'

'Jesus, I dunno. She left it to me. She was Sicilian, that's all I can tell you, all I know.'

'Did she leave anything a message, a letter, some explanation, do you think she knew what it could do?'

'Malloy, I know as much, or as little as you,… oh wait, yeah there was a note attached to it, it said,…'Sofia, see me here as I see you in my heart, always. S.' or something like that, I got a picture of her too, maybe…'

'Sofia, that's your real name isn't it.' Malloy mused.

'Yeah.'

'And her's?'

'Yeah, why? What you getting at?'

'Lucy, maybe it was given to *her* like that, maybe she's the Sofia in question, not you?'

Lucy thought for a second. 'Oh my God Yes,

yes! I see what you mean.'

'Send me a shot of her picture as soon as you can.'

'It's already on my phone, I'll do it now.'

'Good.' Malloy disconnected.

Lucy immediately scrolled through her photos, clicked on a picture of the photograph and sent it to Malloy, along with a message stating the words written on the label.

The door behind Lucy creaked, it was Chinah. 'Aren't you supposed to be at the location to meet Mr Philips?'

'Oh shit.' Lucy clicked off her phone, threw it in her purse and made for the door.

'Chinah call him, tell him I've been delayed, traffic or something.' She flung the words over her shoulder as she ran down the corridor. Chinah caught the door before it closed, went to the computer, and scrolled Lucy's contact list for Michael Philips.

***

The final long-awaited business was on the horizon. Last chapter, books end, retribution attained. But for now, he watched the one who'd be his penultimate creation. It seemed wholly right for it to be her, they had Malloy in common and Escher would enjoy causing him emotional pain, they'd shared Lucy and Escher hated that. He caught sight of his victim again, watched her floral skirt ripple in the breeze and imagined how she'd look as a red head.

TWENTY-FOUR

Malloy clicked the mouse and moved the cursor along the bar, to enlarge the photo Lucy sent of her great aunt.

He'd waited all day to get back to his apartment to do some research. He couldn't do it at work. He was too busy; besides, he didn't want anyone questioning his computer search history.

He stared at the young face of Great Aunt Sofia.

Such an uncanny likeness to Lucy. The same shaped face and nose and her eyes had the same intensity. What're you looking at, what you trying to tell me, Sofia Randazzo.

The great aunt's eyes looked at Malloy, his heart skipped a beat, his hand shot from the mouse as if bee stung, he looked at his fingers and rubbed them one by one hard against his thumb, as if to dispel anything that may have contaminated him. He returned his gaze to the photograph, the malignancy in the photo which his tired eyes had conjured, disappeared.

Coffee that's what I need, coffee, my minds playing tricks…or is it? Maybe this is the norm for me now, seeing weird shit. Maybe the mirror's done something to me? Oh, this is crazy.

He scratched his head, wiped his damp palm on his opposite sleeve and returned his hand to the mouse.

Ok lady, let's see what you're looking at.

He clicked open a new window and typed in… Google maps.

TWENTY-FIVE

'Lucy's late, she's never late.' Kit announced before stuffing a sour cream loaded nacho into her mouth.

Jaz watched, her nose wrinkling in disgust, as the masticated food rolled around inside Kits open orifice.

'Jesus Kit, eat like a normal person, for God's sake close ya mouth n' get your elbows off the table.'

Whilst Jaz and Kit bickered, Chinah used her palm to clear an oval of condensation from the window. She peered through hoping to see the street outside but saw nothing but the reflected interior of the restaurant.

'Where *are you*, Lucy?'

'My dad said men love women with good appetites.' Kit licked the ends of her fingers with rapid little flicks of her tongue.

'Truckers.' Jaz interjected. The word remained airborne for several seconds, an apostrophe between them.

'What about truckers?' Chinah turned her focus back to the girls, her curiosity piqued.

'Kits eating to attract truckers.' Jaz stated, placing a piece of cucumber into her mouth.

'I just said, men like women with good appetites, anyway what's wrong with truckers, I like truckers.' Kit said nibbling her way along a chicken wing.

'Maybe she's forgot, Lucy I mean…' Kit fought to keep the food in her mouth with one hand, whilst she wiped the other on a bib emblazoned with the words 'Fill up at Tanks' in emerald letters. 'Maybe she's seeing that rich guy, that one you set her up with?'

'No, she wasn't interested.' Chinah leant forward, her vast bosoms spreading across the tabletop, like beach stranded jellyfish. 'She thought he was weird.'

'Who gives a shit about weird, the guys loaded. Single straight guy, a heap of cash and no ties.' Kit flung her arms out wide, nearly hitting Chinah in face with the chicken leg she'd just picked up. 'In Manhattan!' She clicked her tongue. 'That's a rarity.' Jaz and Chinah stared at her, eyebrows raised as they waited for the penny to drop.

Kit looked back and forth between them a few times, a little crease between her brows. 'Ooo, I get it. Yeah, I see, you're right, there's gotta be something seriously wrong with him.' The sides of her mouth sprung into a grin. 'You eating that Chi?' She pointed at the remnants of a burrito on Chinah's plate.

'How is it that you ain't fat as a pig?' Chinah said pushing her plate over to Kit. 'Here, go 'head, chow down.'

'Probably all the masturbation.' Jaz offered. Her face expressionless as she munched into her final piece of cucumber.

'What?' Chinah piped up, her forehead crinkling with confusion.

'Burns a lot of calories.' Jaz looked matter-of-factly from Kit to Chinah and back again as though she couldn't understand that they weren't aware of this morsel of information. She leant toward Chinah, so their heads nearly touched.

'Sometimes she does it three times a night.' Jaz's eyes slid sideways and looked accusingly at Kit. Chinah followed suit.

'How the hell do you know?' Kit popped her eyes wide at Jaz and tilted her head in annoyance.

'You make a funny noise when you, er…you

know.' Jaz picked up a length of celery and waved it about before making a big deal of crunching into it.

'But you're all the way down the hall!

'Yeah well, it's a freakin loud funny noise.' Jaz dipped the remnants of the stick into some sour cream and placed it back into her mouth.

Chinah stared at a reddening Kit, with a horrified expression.

'Girl you gots to get a man, and real quick.' She touched Kits hand. 'Real quick sweetie, real quick.' Her eye caught the restaurant clock. 'It ain't like Lucy not to call.' She took her phone from her purse.

'I'm gonna ring her again, see where she's at, maybe somethings happened.' The other two didn't hear, her voice was lost beneath their laughter.

***

A shot of light from the blade made her flinch.

'I'm gonna be nice to you, you know why?' He was close to her ear, close enough to smell her body lotion and the iron in her blood.

The woman didn't reply. No tongue. No words. The blade swept past her eye, she couldn't lean any further from it, so she clenched her lids and held her breath. Heat rose in the back of her throat, she choked and coughed blood onto the stone floor. Dots of bright red hit his shoes. The largest droplet conjoined with others and snaked like gaudy beads of mercury to the floor. He shifted his foot back in line with his other and faced the woman.

'I'm gonna be nice.' He stroked her face lovingly. 'I'm gonna be nice because I'm happy.' He tucked a length of her hair behind her ear, like a lover would. 'You're going to be a gift to her, to show her what she created in me, what she's made me become.'

He flicked away a slither of tongue from her chin.

'Then, I'll be free.'

The woman opened her eyes, and tentatively inched her vision past his blood-spattered shoes and his perfectly pressed trousers. She took in the image of an eagle on his belt buckle and the blue of his expensive shirt and finally his face. Such a handsome face, how could it mask this beast of a man? She wanted to ask why he was doing this, she'd done nothing wrong, nothing to deserve what he'd done to her. But she could not. She felt a scratch on her arm.

'We don't want you to go into heart failure from the shock now do we, that would really defeat the object.'

The drugs entered her body and her thoughts and pain disappeared rapidly into a delicious cotton candy of morphine.

He swapped the needle for a straight blade, gripped her hair and cut away her scalp. As her head lolled, she caught sight of a table next to her, on which lay a curved needle and a red wig. Beyond in a shadow laden corner of the basement was a wooden crate. Before she passed out, she saw, between its slats, the blanched face of a terrified woman.

TWENTY-SIX

Malloy found the church which was in the picture Great Aunt Sophia had given Lucy. He clicked onto street view, roughly calculated the direction in which Sofia was looking, and followed a straight route through the sun-bleached streets until he reached the Museo del Mondo Contadino situated on the opposing hill. He scrolled again to the church, slowly by degrees he turned until he'd completed a full three hundred and sixty, there was no doubt, the only thing she could have been looking at was the museum. Malloy circled his mouse round to bring back the cursor and scrolled down from the map onto the address and other information. Next to a picture of the museum was written…65 photos.

Malloy enlarged the first three one by one, they showed old furniture, antique sewing machines and some patchwork quilts. He scrolled down and randomly clicked on a few others revealing, ancient looking jugs, bowls which were cracked and chipped, old tools, household items and a mirror identical to Lucy's. His hand trembled, he scrubbed the mouse over the picture, until options appeared, he clicked 'save to photos', opened the photo file, found the picture again, clicked and enlarged it one hundred percent, then moved the cursor over the sign, but it was too blurred to make out. Perusing the tool bar, he found the enhance icon, clicked on it and stared at the Italian script. What to do now? Malloy tilted back in his chair, idly studied the cracks in his ceiling and wondered if Sal could help.

Sal was third generation Italian, second generation cop. Recently retired having lost four toes whilst on duty. The official story of how he came to have more room in his loafers was, he'd been caught off guard, whilst on a drugs bust, by a machete wielding gang member. Truth was, Sal was a few steps behind the entry team, when he heard a sound, he turned to see a boy aged about eleven or twelve holding aloft a machete. Before Sal had chance to say or do anything, a skinny scab faced guy jumped in the open window from the adjoining balcony, gun in hand, aimed at Sal. The boy brought down the machete, Sal turned, leaving behind four of his toes and shot scab face through the head, the guy hit the ground, dead. Sal grabbed the machete and threw it next to the guy's free hand. Sal retired soon after, but on occasion he'd work for a private detective agency, this gave him a lot of free time and whenever he got chance, he'd go sit outside Fontaine school around 3pm and watch the boy walk home with his foster mom or sometimes a friend. He didn't blame the kid for what he did, and he never told a soul it wasn't the scab faced guy who'd wielded the machete, the kid deserved a chance and juvie wasn't the place for fresh starts. Sal considered four toes a small price to pay, to save a kid from a life where drugs and crime were as normal as breathing and eating.

Malloy had used Sal before, to obtain info on the down low. But he thought translating a label from a mirror with mystical powers would be too 'out there' for a guy like Sal, so he kept any mention of the supernatural out of his email and made it brief. The least said the better.

Sal, long time no see.
Hope Kate and the kids are well. Do me a solid and translate this.
I'll come over sometime, bring you some beers as

a thanks (and some wine for Kate.)
As long as you keep that dog on a leash, I've still got the teeth marks from the last time!
Stay safe bud.
Garett Malloy.

He clicked send, leant back in his chair, and contemplated sending the picture of the label to Lucy too, but he wasn't sure she knew enough Italian. Besides, he should probably keep things to himself until he was sure what exactly he'd discovered, if anything at all.

He opened a new window and sat for a while watching videos.

Dizzy Gillespie, playing *'And then she stopped.' On Jazz 625. John Coltrane solo, 'Bye Bye Blackbird'* live in Paris and *The Miles Davis Quintet, (The Herbie Hancock years)* performing a rendition of *'Delores.'*

Then halfway through a compilation of cats scared by zucchini, a banner lit up on his monitor.
New email.
It was from Sal.

Hi,
Great to hear from you, Kate says hello and… yes…to the wine. Anytime pal.

Translation you asked for reads…
Replica (Created by local craftsman Giovanni Messi) of a mirror stolen from this museum in 1935.
The mirrored glass and base, (c1900), enclosed a bronze disc with handle. This inner 'mirror' believed to be of ancient Egyptian origin was unearthed in the ruins of the church of Santa Maria (c1395-c1406) on the site of the Castle San Giorgio. Once owned by Francesco 1.

That was all, Malloy sent his thanks in reply and returned to the cats in time to see one jump so high in fright, that it ended up in an empty fruit bowl on its owner's coffee table. He chuckled and ran the cursor back to watch it again.

His phone rang, he rose slowly, numb buttocked from being so long at the computer. The answer machine kicked in as he reached it.

Malloy leave a…

Malloy grabbed the receiver.

'This is Malloy.'

'It's Chinah.'

'Oh, hi how're…'

'Lucy's missing.'

'What do you mean, missing?'

'She was s'posed to meet us, she didn't turn

up, so we've come to her place, the super let us in. We found her phone on the hallway floor, looks like she tried to ring you.'

'Ok, ok, Where and when did you last see her?'

'At work yesterday, she went to meet a client, a man.'

'Ok, have you rung the guy to find out if she turned up to the meeting?'

'Yeah, course, he said she turned up, showed him round the location, he said it was suitable, they'd a brief chat 'bout the best place to get coffee and she left, as far as he knew she'd gone back to the office.'

'Ok, who's there with you now?'

'Just kit, the supers gone.'

Kit grabbed at Chinah's cell phone. 'Give it to me, what's he saying?' Chinah raised it in the air out of reach and pushed Kit in the chest, causing her to stumble backward.

'What the fuck.' Kit protested.

'You're annoying me, I'm trying to think.' Chinah sheep-dogged kit out of the kitchen, using the enormity of her stomach and one outstretched arm. Then closed the door and leant against it.

'We're her family Malloy, she *always* tells us what she's up to and she don't go nowhere without her phone…that just ain't like Lucy.'

'I don't like the sound of this.' Malloy paced between his computer and couch and contemplated what to do next.

Kit pounded her fist on the wooden door. 'Let me in, open the fucking door, I wanna talk to Malloy.'

Chinah held the phone between her breasts, 'Damn it girl can't you keep quiet for one minute?'

'Chinah please!' Kit Pleaded.

Chinah returned the phone to her ear. 'Malloy you gotta do somethin.'

'I think it's something to do with that weirdo Escher.' Kit shouted putting her shoulder to the door and pushing as Chinah shifted her weight.

The door flew open and Kit rushed through snatching the phone from Chinah's hand.

'It's Escher Balodis…' Kit dodged Chinah's attempts to regain the phone. '…works for the New York Wire. He's a weirdo.'

'You wouldn't know a weird guy if he fell on you wearing a hat made o' dicks.' Chinah derided, as she tried to peel the phone from Kits grasp.

Kit spun away managing to keep the phone to her mouth.

'Lucy told me he did weird sex stuff to her.' Kit turned and dangled the cell in front of Chinah. 'There, it's all yours.'

'You know shit, Kit Parker,' Chinah snatched the phone from Kits fingers. 'You been watching too much CSI.'

'I *do* know shit! You! You didn't even know your boyfriend was getting married.'

'What weird stuff, what'd he do to Lucy?' Malloy was getting impatient.

'She slept with him, he did some kinky shit to her, that's all I know.' China said flatly. 'Don't mean he's a bad guy though.'

Malloy's gut churned over. 'Are you sure there's nothing else?'

There were a few moments of silence whilst Chinah mulled over some memories of what Lucy said to her about the night she'd spent with Escher.

She turned away from Kit, cupped her hand over the phone and whispered.

'She said he asked her all sorts of questions 'bout the mirror and…'

'What you saying to him?' Kit said irritated at being left out of the conversation.

Chinah sprang to attention and ran from the kitchen.

Malloy heard nothing but panting and heavy footsteps. 'Chinah you still there?'

Chinah didn't answer, she carried on into the bathroom.

'Chinah! Answer me, what's happening?'

Chinah peered into the bathroom, the dust free circle on the shelf where the mirror had been, zoomed into focus. She put the phone back to her ear.

'The mirrors gone.' Her voice quivered slightly. 'I think Kit's right, I think Escher's taken it, it could be something to do with Jim Carrera.'

'Who the fucks Jim Carrera?' Malloy could feel his heart pounding faster with each minute.

'He's a Medium, a supernatural entertainer, I got a…a friend, Calvin, who works for the New York Wire, he was quizzing me about supernatural shit, his boss wants to run some articles to boost interest in Jim's tour.'

Kit appeared next to Chinah in the bathroom doorway and looked around the room wondering what was getting Chinah so freaked out.

'What's happening?' She poked Chinah in the shoulder.

Chinah shrugged her away.

'You think, maybe Escher stole the mirror for this Jim Carrera?' Malloy asked.

'How long you been a cop, keep up God dammit, yes, an' if he stole the mirror, then maybe he stole Lucy too, she said it don't seem to work for no-one else but her.'

Malloy knew that Chinah was right, the mirror did only respond to Lucy.

'Don't worry, I'll find her.' Malloy ended the call and thought how crazy it all sounded, but crazy seemed to be the norm these days. Putting his cell in his pocket he grabbed his car keys and made for the door.

A thought popped into his head; *if a reporter got their hands on the mirror, they'd have every unsolved mystery at their finger tips. That'd bring fame and fortune for sure.*

Chinah stared at her dead cell.

'Whaaaaaat...' Kit tried to shake Chinah, but only succeeded in wobbling her triceps '...is happening?'

Chinah sat down on the side of Lucy's tub and pointed at the toilet seat. 'Sit down, you're not gonna fuckin believe what I'm about to tell ya.'

TWENTY-SEVEN

Malloy flung open the door to his Buick and dove into the seat. The thing about having a ride as old as the hills and as exciting as soda water, was no-one in their right mind wanted to steal it. He started the engine and pulled out. An indecipherable mass of thoughts regarding Lucy and Escher, whirled around his head, as if he were watching mis-matched socks in a washer.

Do I call it in? What proof have I got?...Nada, just hearsay and a bunch of voodoo that nobody's gonna believe.

He decided to ring Cable.

'I need an address.'

'What makes you think...' Cable started, annoyed at Malloys lack of politeness at such a late hour.

'Damn it Cable, I need it now.'

'Who?'

'Balodis, first name Escher.'

'Unusual name, should be easy.'

There were a few seconds of silence.

'8 Jay Street Tribeca.'

'Apartment?'

'It's the whole damn building, Jeez, must be one rich son of a bitch…'

Malloy, cut him off, threw his phone on the passenger seat and took a right, swerved round a car and continued, pursued by the blare of its horn. He approached lights, the car in front anticipated a red and stopped. Malloy slammed on his brakes.

'Fuck, come on, come on.' He pounded his palm into the steering wheel, before pulling left, foot hard on the accelerator he careered across the intersection. He tensed and squinted his right eye as the sound of brakes screeched toward his passenger side, the Nissan swerved only missing Malloy's vehicle by inches, the momentum sent its back-end skidding in a wide arc, Malloy watched in his rear-view mirror as the car following crashed into it, shunting the vehicle another fifteen feet or so down the road.

'Fuuuck.' His spittle flew on to the dash.

He pressed on toward Tribeca. Wondering what he was going to do and say about this damn magic mirror when he saw Escher.

As if there's not enough crazy bastards in this city, I'm now one of them.

He wiped a bead of sweat away as it approached his eye.

A sudden shock of adrenaline pricked his cheeks, *what if Escher were more than just some rich nut who believed the mirror had…*

He wrangled with the word in his head, not wanting to add it to his thoughts, but it popped out.

Power, yeah, some freakin weird power.

He rang Cable again.

'What the fuck Garret?'

'Listen, I owe you one, I need info on this Balodis guy and now.'

Cable gave an audible sigh. 'Ok, I'm on it.'

Malloy kept the line open as he continued through Soho. The place was alive, diners and clusters of party goers shuffled in disorderly lines outside the high-end restaurants and nightspots. Some sauntered along gazing through windows at the artwork in the many galleries, or at pricey designer outfits fitted to impossibly skinny mannequins in the exclusive boutiques. He drove past the spot where he'd first met Mel, she'd been on a girl's night out, he, with colleagues on a bachelor night. He remembered walking behind her, admiring her great ass, she'd stopped abruptly, he hadn't, there were apologies, some flirting, and his crass but well received pick-up line. The two groups mingled, chatted, then headed to the same club. In a dark nook, Mel, drunk on cheap champagne, gave him his first lap dance. That was it, he was captivated.

Malloy drove on for a second, a hint of a smile across his face, then unexpectedly and like a series of paintings in a macabre art display, images flashed through his head. The angled knitting needle, the look on her face, the hospital waiting room. He shook his head, God he'll never till his dying day forget that look. For a microsecond he screwed up his eyes, hoping his lids would act as blackout curtains to the glare of memories.

'Malloy, you listening?' Cables voice broke through to him.

'Yeah, what you got?'

'Ok, drug addicted mom, currently wanted for parole violation, whereabouts unknown. Father unknown, no known relatives. Suffered physical, sexual and psychological abuse as a child. Entered care aged six. Suffered from PTSD, treatment for schizoid personality disorder, yada yada yada.

'Picture?'

'Of the mom yes, him no.'

Malloy thought for a second.

'Try the Internet.'

Malloy continued down Varick toward Tribeca.

God Lucy, I hope you're somewhere stupid, visiting a friend, someone new, someone the girls don't know. Just not with this guy.

'Malloy.'

'Yup.'

'I'm sending it through.'

'Thanks, I owe you.'

'I'll add it to your tab.'

Malloy huffed, 'Night Cable.' Malloy touched the red icon and closed his phone.

Minutes later he pulled up outside Escher's building.

TWENTY-EIGHT

Lucy struggled to her feet, unsteady, as if she were on a tight rope for the first time. She grabbed the hefty slats of the wooden crate and waited for her head to catch up with her body, and for the nausea to subside. Eventually she lifted her head, opened her eyes and saw Escher in the centre of the room.

He stood over a beaten rag doll of a woman who was tied to a chair. Lucy glanced about the room, on the far side were more wooden crates like the one she was in, they stood empty and foreboding on the periphery of the ochre light. The floor around was bare, there were no windows and the room smelled too dank to be anything other than a basement. As her eyes adjusted to the dim light, she was able to survey the crate she was in, the wood smelled new and it was obviously built in-situ, as it was too large to have been brought in through the small doorway in the wall opposite.

A gurgle made Lucy look up. Escher held the woman's hair and was cutting away a section of her scalp with a straight razor. Although sickened at the sight, Lucy could not take her eyes from the scene. Escher continued slicing until he'd removed the remainder of the woman's hair and scalp, he wiped her face with a rag to remove the excess blood and threw the bloodied fabric to the floor. Next, he took up the upholstery needle which lay on a table by his side stared at it for several seconds before putting it back down. He picked up the wig opened it out and fit it to the woman's head, moving it about and ducking side to side, like a hairdresser checking the symmetry of his clients bangs. Satisfied with its position, he picked up the gun tacker and punched a line of staples through the wig into the woman's head front to back and side to side, tugged to check it was secure and finally, stepped back to admire his creation.

'Almost done, got to make her just right.' He twisted round to face the crate. 'Haven't we Lucy?'

Every muscle in Lucy's body formed into knots, as his eyes bored into her.

She opened her mouth to plead with him to stop what he was doing, but no words came out, just a throaty rasp.

'Don't worry.' He soothed. 'We're friends, you and I, I'm not going to hurt you.' He took a step toward her. 'That's not what you're here for.' He placed the gun tacker onto the table and folded his arms. 'You've never had a child, you've never broken the unspoken promise of motherhood, you don't deserve to die, like her.' He nodded toward the woman. 'She had children; did she look after them?' He twisted his neck rapidly, producing an audible click, then repeated the movement to the other side. 'No, she got a nanny five days a week so she could work, and weekends the kids went to Nanna and Grandpa's whilst she and her fancy damn husband went to the golf club to have drinks with friends.' He ran his fingers through his hair and refolded his arms. Lucy noticed his hands squeezing his biceps as though he were desperately trying to control himself.

'That bitch…' A glob of frothy white spittle launched from his mouth and landed on the concrete floor near Lucy, its tiny bubbles popping randomly as it dissolved into the dust.

'…*she* took children that were not hers and then gave birth to her own *knowing* they would suffer in a world where hate and abuse hide… in…every…corner and she wasn't there to protect them. SHE SHOULD BE PUNISHED, FOR HER SELFISHNESS.'

Lucy's heart felt ready to explode with terror. Escher swirled away, picked up the razor, grabbed the woman's lower lip and sliced the blade across it. The pink flesh came away in his hand and he threw it onto the table. Quickly he swapped blade for gun. As the first staple went into the woman's jaw, it created a pain even the drugs could not dampen, she sprang to life with a boar like bellow, blood spewing from her mouth, legs flailing helplessly as she twisted from side to side.

'Stop it, stop it.' Lucy screamed.

'Stop it? I can't stop it, you're the only one who can stop it.' Escher put down the staple gun. 'Lucy…, grandniece of Sofia Lucia Randazzo.'

The woman gurgled and squirmed behind him. He took a step toward Lucy. '…the one who stole the mirror of Santa Lucia from the museum del Mondo…'

Lucy froze.

'…she stole it, no doubt after discovering its powers and used it to watch over her lover, Severu Amato.'

Lucy remembered the letter attached to the mirror.

Sophia, see me here as I see you in my heart. Always S.

Malloy was right. The message wasn't for me, it was left by Severu!

Escher drew close to her, a skewed grin contorting his face.

'I wonder if she knew he was a fascist Blackshirt, maybe she watched as the mustard gas he'd planned to use on innocent villagers, burnt and blistered his skin. Maybe she even heard his lungs rattle as it liquified their lining.' Escher reached above Lucy out of her line of vision. 'Maybe she watched it happen in this.'

He placed her great aunts mirror in-front of Lucy's face.

Lucy saw her fear reflected.

'How, how'd you find out?'

'I've got money Lucy, it's easy to send someone…,' he raised an eyebrow, tilted his head and continued.

'…a discreet someone, to enquire about an old lady in a village, a village where people love to gossip, it's easy…child's play.'

He reached into his pocket and pulled out a black and white crimp edged photograph. 'And now you're gonna find this woman for me.' Escher pinned the top of the picture against the horizontal wooden slat above Lucy's head with his index finger and let the remainder dangle in front of her face. A young woman, hollow cheeked and dark eyed stared solemnly at Lucy.

'What so you can do that to her?' Lucy nodded toward the woman.

'No, there's something special I have in mind for this one.' He lifted the mirror and held it at an angle so that both he and Lucy could see the glass.

'Ask it where she is, and I'll let you go.'

Lucy looked at him suspiciously, his expression gave away no hint of a lie, *she knew as a killer and a psychotic one at that, he could probably say the earths flat and be totally believable.*

'What assurances have I got?' She narrowed her eyes.

'None…but then again it's not like you've got options.'

'I could refuse.' A trickle of perspiration ran down Lucy's forehead and dripped from her nose.

She crooked her finger and wiped away the itch it left behind.

'Believe me, fifty of this woman…' He tapped the picture. 'ain't worth one of you, I don't want to have to *make* you help me Lucy, and I can make you, as you see, I have certain talents.' He fabricated a smile. 'Please Lucy, for both our sakes.'

Lucy thought for a second and decided she had no choice. Maybe whoever the woman was, would be gone by the time Escher reached her location.

'What's her name?'

Escher bowed his head. 'Mariam…Mariam Balodis.' He forced the words out, as if they were glued inside him.

'Balodis, but that's your name…'

'Ask it the fucking question!'

Lucy sucked on her cheeks, swallowed, took a good look at the photograph, and addressed the mirror.

'Where is Mariam Balodis?'

She and Escher stared at the glass. Lucy realised their breathing had become synchronised; it didn't feel right that she had even that in common with him, she held her breath purposefully and began her own rhythm.

The glass misted; Lucy hoped the mirror wouldn't be too exacting.

A section on the right side of the mirror revealed some metal poles, then coloured fabric.

Lucy was relieved, so far it seemed vague.

Escher adjusted his grip on the mirror and as Lucy began to hope his plan had been thwarted, the remainder of the mist cleared and a number as plain as if Lucy had written it herself was displayed across the mirror. 1441, behind it was an unmistakable image of Time square.

Escher recognised the scene from photographs in the New York Wire.

'She's camping out with the Time Square vagrants!' A sneer of smugness crossed his face.

He returned the photo to his pocket, reached through one of the slats and stroked Lucy's cheek.

'Good girl.'

In an eye blink Lucy twisted her head, clamped her teeth onto his index finger and bit down as hard as she could, the taste of liquid iron spurted into her mouth. Quickly she reached through the bars, grabbed Escher's sleeve under his armpit with her right hand, took his wrist with her left and spat his blood into his face.

Escher dropped the mirror to the floor; it made a metallic clank and a slight crunch as the glass cracked. He drew his loose hand across his eyes, wiped away the blood and jerked his trapped arm in an attempt to extract it. Lucy's grip was resolute, in a split second she braced her foot against the slats, jumped, twisted and pushed down on his arm, as she landed there was a loud pop as Escher's elbow dislocated.

'Argh! You fucking bitch.' He punched at the wood with his good fist and yanked out his injured arm.

Lucy stepped away from the front of the crate as quickly as she could, her heart beating fiercely.

Escher felt the electric buzz of adrenaline spit needles into his blood. Too incensed to pause and open the lock, he kicked and punched at the horizontal wooden slats, slavering, and bawling like a beast, several bars gave way and Escher was able to step through and reach Lucy as she cowered in the corner.

With his uninjured arm he grabbed her by the throat, the impetus took her off her feet. He pulled her to him, snarled in her face, then thrust her backward against the rear of the crate, the curve of her skull hit the solid wall behind the slats, pain, and the sickening sound her head made against the brick resonated through Lucy's body. Escher took in a deep breath, released his grip and let Lucy slump to the floor.

Her head was full of thunder, and flecks of light blurred her vision like grains of silica thrown into the sun's rays.

Escher looked at his strangely angled elbow.

'I gotta fix this, then I'm going to find her.' He paused a beat, made a fist with his good hand, swooped down and punched Lucy into darkness.

TWENTY-NINE

Malloy peered through the first-floor window of Escher's building. The only movement inside were the blinking circles of sapphire and ruby stand-by lights, tucked away in the recesses of the room.

Stepping back, he rubbed his neck and wondered whether to ring the bell and confront Escher.

'He's not in.' The elderly woman, matted wig askew was rifling through a nearby trash can. 'Went out at five, ain't come back yet.'

'You sure?'

'Sure as I shit in the street I am.' She pulled out a newspaper, sniffed it, tucked it in her waistband and waddled off.

Malloy's phone rang. It was Chinah.

'You found her yet?'

'No. Not yet, but I will.' A thought popped into Malloy's head. 'What was the name of the guy she went to meet?'

'Micheal…Philips, why?'

'You got his number?

'Yeah, hang on.' Chinah scrolled through Lucy's phone. 'Here it is, 5550102.'

'Ok, I'll let you know, soon as I find her.' Malloy disconnected and keyed in the number she'd given him, listening to the tone as he held his breath. It began to ring, Malloy waited, no one answered, he cut off the call and rang again, still no luck. It was then he realised there was a ringing nearby, which had stopped both times he'd disconnected. He rang again moving closer to the sound coming from inside the apartment. He approach the window, pressed his nose against the glass and watched as an oblong of grey light shone from a cell phone on the table inside. Malloy cut the call and the light went out… *shit, what the hell's going on? Why would this guy, Escher, pretend to be Michael Philips, why would…?* A sudden realisation hit him. *Maybe Lucy wouldn't date you again, so you pretended to be a client, forced her back to her apartment and got the mirror…then where did you take her, where?*

He could think of only one place, the movie location.

His phone gave out a short thrum, it was an incoming email from Cable, he crossed the sidewalk, jumped into his car, and turned the key in the ignition. Malloy held his phone against the steering wheel and tapped to open the attachment, as he pulled away, a newspaper picture of a suited sinewy man, revealed itself on the screen. There was a headline, something about entrepreneur of the year, he scrolled down to the other picture Cable had sent. A woman, her features wizened and hollow, head surrounded by gaudy red hair, lips so utterly thin and pale it seemed as though she had none at all. Below the picture Cable had written. Mariam Balodis.

Malloy rammed the accelerator, tyres screeched leaving deposits of black rubber lining the road.

In a flash it became clear, the killer had seen the article in the Wire giving him the pseudonym Jagger, the real Mick Jagger was born Michael Philip Jagger. Malloy had established Escher was Michael Philips, so therefore Escher was the Jagger.

Lucy was in trouble, much more trouble than he'd first imagined. As he careered through the streets back the way he'd come, he contemplated calling for backup, but it occurred to him if they arrived before he did, Escher would be cornered, and Lucy could be in mortal danger. The image of Escher blowing first Lucy's, then his own brains out, flashed through Malloy's mind. The prostitutes and addicts Escher murdered deserved retribution, but if it meant saving Lucy, Malloy was prepared to set Escher free.

***

Malloy's Buick came to a halt outside the vacant buildings. He got out and circled the exterior looking for a way in. Down a short drive he found a gate slightly ajar, but jammed against the ground, he put his shoulder against it, pushed hard several times and it flung open. Malloy stumbled through colliding with a large planter which contained a dried up and long dead shrub.

He paused and listened wondering if he'd been heard, but there was nothing except the usual background thrum of the city. He steadied himself before stepping as quietly as he could around the perimeter of the main building. Coming to a dark blue rust-edged door he tried the handle, it was locked. He continued along the wall, peering in at the edges of every window, seeing nothing but dim reflected lights from the buildings opposite.

He rounded a corner, several yards away he spied a two-storey building much older than the others, it was in a bad state, the mortar was crumbling and there were holes where bricks had fallen out, sometimes several in one area. The only entrance was a large wooden door hanging open at an odd angle, held to its frame by a solitary hinge. Malloy ran across and stepped through it, into the sanctuary of the building's darkness.

Fishing in his pocket, he took out a small flashlight and pointed it slightly forward of his feet, the floor here seemed solid enough. Before stepping further inside he zigzagged the circle of light slowly around the room, illuminating piles of wooden doors stacked against the side walls. Old pieces of abandoned machinery and piles of boxes in varying shades of grey littered almost the entirety of the remaining space. Malloy turned to leave, took a step and clicked off the flash, as the light disappeared, he thought he saw something in the dirt. He turned the flash on again and shone it around his feet until it picked out a thin length of red fibre, shiny-new and out of place. He picked it up, laid it in his hand and shone the flashlight directly on it. His heart thumped in his chest as he saw it was a long red fibre from a wig.

Using the torch to slice through the dark he walked further through the storage area to the far wall but found nothing. A dead end. As he turned to retrace his steps, he spied a black square on the ground behind one of the machines, he walked closer, and saw it was an entrance to a set of steps leading downward, the wooden hatch door was open, propped against the back of the machine. No-one would have known it was there unless they'd worked at the place or had seen the plans to the site. Malloy put the torch momentarily in the crook of his neck and held it with his chin whilst he took out his gun and released the safety. He took the torch in his spare hand and slowly descended the steps into a dry, brick-lined corridor. Ahead a light shone from a doorway.

'Escher.' Malloy waited a couple of seconds for a reply or a sound of any kind. Nothing.

'Escher, I know you're here, I wanna make a deal.' He continued to walk the corridor, alert to each darkened arch and doorway. As he approached the light, he switched off his torch and placed it in his pocket.

'I know what your mother did to you…she should be punished…but Lucy's innocent, she's a victim Escher, just like you.'

Malloy stopped and leant against the wall next to the door whilst his eyes adjusted to the brighter light coming from the room.

'I'm coming in.' He waited two beats before he

sprang into the doorway.

A single strip light lit the room, and on its periphery, he saw a female figure slumped against the front of a broken freight crate, her head lolled at a strange angle, and blood, in congealed lumps, clung to her disfigured face. Malloy holstered his gun and ran forward.

'Lucy! Oh my God what's he done to you.' The body began to slide sideways. Malloy managed to get his hand underneath her head before it hit the ground. As soon as her flesh touched his skin, he knew she was dead. He leant his forehead on her shoulder, ran his hand down her arm and interlaced his fingers with hers.

A cloak of ice, nausea and loss enveloped him. He squeezed her hand tightly and felt something cold, much colder than dead skin. He brought her hand up to his face and stared at the gold band on her ring finger. He frowned in confusion, then in his mind a spark of hope ignited, lowering her hand and head gently to the ground he swiftly took off his T-shirt and used it to clean as much of the blood from her face as was possible. He stared at her features and tried to compare them to his memory of Lucy, but there was too much swelling and discolouration to be certain of the shape of anything. Malloy took out his phone, to call the precinct, that's when he saw the tattoo on the inside of her wrist, a small heart, perfect except for a central star of un-inked flesh. He rotated his forearm and stared with sadness at his red star tattoo, he took her hand in his, their wrists touched, and the heart and star became one.

'A star to fill your heart with light.' He leant forward and kissed the blood-streaked cheek of the woman who was once his wife.

THIRTY

A line of clothes and bedding hung from the scaffold surrounding the vacant store on the south side of west 41st, between 7th and Broadway. The vagrants forced uncommonly together by torrential rain the previous night, lay beneath the sheltering span of scaffold planks, high above them.

So far police had turned a blind eye to the gathering, having better things to attend to in such a busy city.

Most slept huddled under blankets and cardboard. Several new to the streets tossed and turned, denied their rest by the LED panels lately installed on Ball drop tower which pulsed rainbows of colour tormentingly across their eyelids. Some lay awake, unable to sleep, disturbed by the ghosts of lives past. One, Mariam, slept deeply, there was nothing that troubled or frightened her, nothing that anyone could ever do to her that had not already been done a thousand times over. The night cradled her, darkness forgave her, and sleep offered her succour.

A few yards away in the darkened doorway of Ruby Tuesdays, Escher perused the row of shambolic bodies and wondered how he could discover which lump of rags shared his DNA.

On the periphery of the undulating huddle, sat a mass of tangled hair and beard. The body to which it belonged was hunched inside a tent-like overcoat of greasy canvas. Every minute or so, a hand appeared from the sleeve to deliver a slug of something satisfying to the lips, hidden among the forest of a face. Escher slipped out of his hiding place and took the quickest route over to sit against the vacant wall, nearest the hirsute individual.

The two ignored each other for several minutes and then as Escher was about to speak, a voice came from behind the hair.

'S'pose you want summin?' The man turned to Escher. 'People never come close unless they want summin, I know you ain't one of them religious freaks, not this time o'night.'

'I'm looking for someone.'

'Ain't we all.'

'Someone I knew a long time ago, her name's Mariam.'

'Don't know no-one with that name.'

'I can help, maybe with a finder's fee?' Escher brought a twenty from his pocket, he didn't proffer it to the vagrant, but folded it in half lengthways and ran the nails of his thumb and forefinger along the edge to straighten it out.

'Seems your friends not worth finding.' The man focussed on the twenty.

Escher pulled another bill from his pocket and repeated the straightening process.

The head disappeared down the neck of the overcoat and to Escher's surprise there was a whispered conversation between two people, or it may have been just the bearded man and his other self, there was no way of knowing. The head popped out again.

'What's she look like?'

Escher bit hard onto his lower lip, a miniature red balloon of blood formed, he sucked it into his mouth and a memory flashed through him of days when the taste of blood was frequent.

'Red hair, thin lips, grey eyes…'

'That'll be Em, Ok, ok.' He said and patted a lump in the fabric before holding his hand out to Escher. 'Light blue blanket.' Escher deposited the promised dollars into the cruddy palm and picked his way carefully along the sidewalk.

Two thirds down the line of bodies, Escher spied the light blue blanket, he bent down and lifted it slightly. It was undeniably her. Multi coloured lights trailed across the gaunt structure of her face, lending it a macabre glow. Escher took out his phone and dialled, he let it ring three times then disconnected the call. It was past four in the morning and still people were out in the street, most chose the opposite side of the road and followed their feet or the sidewalk with their eyes, purposely ignoring the vagrants.

After a glance around, Escher stepped back against one of the vertical scaffolding poles and slid down next to the feet protruding from the blue blanket. The other bodies who shared the area, purred and snorted. Escher reached into his pocket, found the syringe he'd prepared and popped the top off with his thumb. On his knees he sidled the length of her, took in a breath and readied himself for the strike. In one slick move he circled her head clamping her chin with his hand, forcing it back to prevent her from screaming and at the same time plunged the needle into her neck. For a split second the woman's eye's popped wide open, then just as quickly rolled back into her head, slowly her lids closed. A few feet away a vehicle came to a stop, its window wound down. Escher looked up momentarily startled.

'Perfect timing.' He said with relief. 'Gimme a hand.'

'Hey, what you doing!' A bedraggled woman a few bodies away woke, she prodded the sleepers around her, some remained motionless, some slowly stirred. 'The bastards are taking Em!'

The driver sprang from his seat. 'Quick.' Escher urged. The two men lifted Mariam's limp body into the back seat and jumped into the car as the shouting woman leapt onto the hood. The force of the moving car flung her aside and Escher watched her reel away, stumbling into blankets and bodies before finally falling backward and disappearing among the waking.

On a quiet side street several blocks away the vehicle pulled up, the two men got out, Escher went to the trunk and wrapped the limp body more securely in the blanket before he transferred it to his car.

'There's the five…' He placed a large wad of money in the hand of his accomplice and shook it. 'I'm leaving tomorrow, don't forget our deal, no cops, the money we agreed on will go into your bank account each year.'

'Five years.' The guy stated as he counted the money.

'Five years'

'Nice doin business wij ya.' The guy nodded to Escher and held up the money.

Escher ignored him, slammed shut the trunk of his car and let an irresistible smirk lift his top lip.

THIRTY-ONE

Malloy looked at the mangled mess of the woman he once loved and gently covered her face with his t-shirt.

He laboured to stand, stumbled against the wall to steady himself and retched. A thud in the corridor put him on pause.

Lucy?

He was about to shout her name again, when something small and diamond like a few feet from him caught his eye. He squinted and realised it was a shard of mirror glass. Another noise came from the corridor, this time a scraping sound. Malloy braced himself and took out his gun. The noise outside continued, he aimed toward the grey corridor and waited. A person hunched over and pulling on the ankles of a body entered the room backward.

Malloy stepped into the light aiming his thirty-eight ahead of him. 'Police, hands in the air.'

The figure instantly let go of the legs, they hit the floor heavily, causing a faint groan to come from the body.

The person turned to face Malloy, staring at him with dead fisheyes.

'Escher Balodis.'

'Yes, that's correct, officer Malloy, I do believe we have…' he paused for a self-gratifying grin, 'had…the lovely Lucy and of course your dear ex-wife in common'. He signalled to Mel's body and took a step toward Malloy. 'Unfortunately, I miscalculated her meds, shame, I'd hoped to keep her alive a little longer.'

'Stay where you are.'

'Where I am?' Escher threw out his arms. 'No, you see…' He shrugged his shoulders. 'Garret, isn't it? I can't stay where I am because I have a very important…task, to perform.' He gestured toward the body which he'd been dragging.

Malloy looked at the blanket and realised the feet and legs sticking out were old and thread veined and definitely not Lucy's.

'Where's Lucy, you better not have hurt her… you sick twisted fuck.' Malloy gritted his teeth, his knuckles blanched as his fingers tightened around the grip of his gun. He took a few steps toward Escher.

'Ah, poor Lucy, too late for that pretty little thing, if you're wondering, I didn't do *that*...' He pointed to Malloy's ex-wife. '...to her, if that's what you're worried about, she was never meant to be one of my...creations.'

Malloy's blood burned, he charged toward Escher and smashed him across the face with the back of his gunned hand. Escher flew against the wall, recoiled, and lunged at Malloy grabbing his wrists and head butting him in the face. Blood exploded from Malloy's nose, he twisted his wrist round to point his gun at Escher, then realised he needed him alive to find Lucy. Throwing his leg back, he brought his knee forward and smashed it into Escher's testicles, the pain ripped through Escher's groin, forcing him to release his grip enough for Malloy to be able to pull away.

Malloy smashed his gun-butt into Escher's temple, completing the onslaught with a kick to Escher's kneecap. Escher growled and doubled up in pain, Malloy's fist came up under his jaw and Escher stumbled back collapsing onto the dirt floor, Malloy pounced on Escher, straddling him and pinning his arms beneath his shins, causing Escher to howl in pain as his elbow popped once more under the weight of Malloy. Malloy grabbed Escher round the neck and pressed the barrel of his gun to his forehead.

'Where is she? You bag of shit. Where is she!'

Escher's eyes steeled into Malloy's.

'She's in the Hudson, I slit her throat with a straight blade, she didn't struggle for long.' He smiled as he thought of Malloy waiting days, expecting Lucy's body to surface somewhere along the river. It never would.

Malloy's face screwed with pain and anger, he tossed his gun aside and pummelled into Escher's face with his fists, bones crunched, blood sprayed, Malloy paused momentarily, his breath heavy from the exertion.

Escher lifted his head, spat out tooth and blood and screamed into Malloy's face.

'LET'S PUT SOME EFFORT INTO IT, SHALL WE?'

Malloy grabbed Escher's throat again and pulled back his fist to continue the beating, he paused, Escher was staring over his shoulder, terror in his eyes. Malloy spun his head round, a skeletal red-haired woman, eyes like golf balls, teeth bared, stood behind him. In her hand was a brick, she smashed it into Malloy's face, and he crumpled to the floor.

The woman pounced across Escher, picked up Malloy's gun and held it triumphantly.

Escher lifted himself onto his good elbow and tried to shuffle back toward the doorway.

'No momma, please don't momma, please don't.'

His mother smiled, Escher closed his eyes tightly and whimpered. She aimed and squeezed the trigger, Malloy twitched violently as the bullet ripped through his head. Escher opened his eyes and watched the cops body go limp as dark blood oozed from the bullet hole.

Mariam checked how many bullets were left in the barrel, clicked the safety on and then knelt at the side of her son.

'All those years babba.' She brushed back his hair.

'I deserved what I got, for not doing nuthin to stop it. I shoulda killed myself, I shoulda killed us both, saved us from what they done.'

Escher stared at her and tried to make sense of what she was telling him.

'When that woman cop found us and took you away, it was the best thing coulda happened, you made sumthin of yourself, you got rich, you showed 'em babba.'

She tucked the gun into her waistband and helped her dumbstruck son slowly to his feet, and together they made their way out from the underground store.

Up top, faint light beckoned to them from the doorway on the far side of the warehouse. With the gait of a new-born deer, Mariam loped ahead, to check there was no-one in the courtyard outside. Meanwhile Escher wended his way slowly to the door, pausing several times to steady himself against the machinery. Behind him a dot-to-dot string of blood droplets lay suspended momentarily before being absorbed, one by one into the dust. He finally caught up with Mariam, and together they made their way through the buildings followed by the thin straw-coloured light of dawn. They continued on to where Escher's rented Prius was parked. He passed Mariam a set of keys from his pocket and without a word she took them and got into the driver's side. Escher slid carefully into the passenger seat cradling his arm, as his adrenaline levels began to decline, so the intensity of his pain increased, the throbbing was almost unbearable, Escher's face looked drained and sweaty.

'Here take this.' Mariam passed him a wrap.

'What is it?' Escher took the tiny parcel of white powder and looked at it suspiciously.

'It'll stop the pain, take it.' She pulled out of the parking space. 'Where to?'

Escher sniffed some of the powder and felt it

burn along his sinuses.

'Somewhere I can think.' He twisted the top of the wrap to secure the remainder of the powder. 'Things haven't worked out the way I'd planned.'

THIRTY-TWO

Chinah and Kit followed the dots of blood that led from the building behind the old UPS distribution centre.

'Oh my God Kit, you were right, I'm gonna ring the police.'

'I told you they'd be here.' Kit and Chinah followed the drops further into the disused warehouse. 'Ring Malloy again.' Kit pointed to Chinah's phone.

'I did, he's still not answering.' Chinah dialled 9 then caught sight of Kit. 'What the hell are you doing?'

Kit had found the open hatch and already had a foot on the top step.

'Goin down.'

'Don't be an idiot.' Chinah implored. 'I'm calling the cops.'

Kit paused for a second, as she contemplated

what to do. Daylight spread in from the window, its fuzzy fingers caught a stack of rusty tools and metal bars which leant against the wall. Kit stared at them for a second, then taking her foot from the step, she walked over to the pile, chose a sturdy shaft, shook it in her fist then slapped it against her palm.

'This'll do.' She said triumphantly.

'Do for what?'

'I dunno just in case.'

'Yep, that's a great idea, follow a crazy guy into a hole in the ground.' Chinah gasped.

'Could be they've left, look how the drops get smaller toward the exit.' Kit pointed at the decreasing trail of blood toward the warehouse door.'

'Oh my god Kit, You're NOT fucking Columbo, wait for the cops.' Chinah implored as she dialled the final two digits.

Kit peered down the stairwell.

'We gotta check it out, make sure she's not down there injured. Lucy we're coming.' Kit shouted into the hole. She looked up and caught sight of Chinah's terrified face, 'ok' she said smacking her palm with the bar once more. *'I'm coming.'* She shouted descending the steps.

'911 What's your emergency?'

'What?' Chinah suddenly remembered she'd dialled. 'Oh, yes, emergency, my friends been kidnapped, he wants her mirror to help a magician.' Chinah cringed when she heard her words out loud.

Below her, Kit continued into the corridor, creeping slowly toward the faint light at the far end, above her she caught part of China's conversation.

'Yeah, it's a magic mirror, that's what I said… no I'm serious…Hello. Hello?'

Several seconds later Kit felt Chinah's presence behind her. 'There's no cops, just us.' Chinah whispered.

Kit pulled a sneer. 'Magic mirror, seriously, you might well have said King Kong, and the Mummy are helping us find her.' She tutted, 'Freakin magic mirror.'

They reached the open door. Kit held aloft the metal bar and mouthed to Chinah. One, two, three. She pounced into the room, Chinah followed her, eyes wide, scared as a mouse.

Malloy lay face up on the floor, blood pooling around his head and shoulders, part of his skull was missing and some of what Kit reasoned to be brain, lay in a gloopy blob, a grey island in a sea of red.

Chinah gagged, threw up and ran from the room. Kit placed her hand over her mouth and nose and retched, partly from the sight of Malloy and partly from the stench of China's semi digested pancakes.

She turned away from the horrific vision and her eyes alighted on something else which made her scream.

Chinah quickly wiped her mouth on her sleeve and staggered back into the doorway, in the half light on the far side of the room, she saw Kit on her knees, a blood-soaked female form by her side.

'Oh my God, is that, is that Lucy.'

'I dunno, it could be, I hope not.' Kit carefully peeled the t-shirt from the head of the body, revealing an unrecognisable face beneath a red wig.

Chinah let out a mewl and slid down into a heap, she took out her phone intending to call the cops again, but it was difficult, her eyes were blurred with tears and her hands were shaking.

Kit looked around the room. There were several wooden crates, a chair with ropes tied to the arms and back, a small table on which lay a staple gun and some other macabre looking bloody instruments. On the floor a few yards away from her, she saw the mirror. She staggered over and picked it up, careful not to cut herself on the broken glass.

'Lucy's dead because of this stupid thing.' She screamed with anger and threw it across the room.

Chinah held her cell phone shakily 'I want t' to report.' She gulped back a surge of grief. 'I want to report a, a double murder.'

THIRTY-THREE

Lucy forced open her dust laden eyelids, around her, laces of light struggled through gaps in the broken brickwork and dissipated into the black-coffee darkness. She lay still for a moment, to evaluate her physical condition. Her head throbbed, her right arm was numb from being trapped between her ribs and the dirt floor, she touched her cheek gingerly with her working hand and was amazed that it wasn't more swollen considering the blow she'd received.

Twisting herself to free her arm, she felt fresh blood flow into it, nipping and stinging its way along her arteries. A sudden loud bang from above resonated around the cramped chamber. Lucy scrunched herself into a ball as much as she could, froze and held her breath until she was sure nothing about her was going to collapse.

'Help, HELP!' Lucy tried to move around, to

get her face nearer to gaps where the light came in, but there was not enough space. Turning her head ever so slightly from side to side she listened for voices. All she could hear was a faint grinding interspersed with the sound of an engine, the noise grew louder, the bricks and rubble about her began to shake.

She attempted to scream for help again, but plumes of dust whipped in from outside, dried her throat and caused her to emit nothing but a feeble choke.

THIRTY-FOUR

Mariam and Escher walked silently together through the park for what seemed like ages. Initially each focussed on their individual physical and mental pain, then without prompting Mariam began to unravel the story of her youth, her drug dependence, the men who used her, and how she'd tried to protect Escher when he was a child, she explained the things she'd said to him and the way she behaved, was to make him strong, to harden him to the life from which they couldn't escape. When the police found them, she was too weak physically and mentally to fight any more. She took some of the blame for what happened to him, she knew at the time it was best for them to be separated, best that he was taken away, given a new start.

She went to prison willingly, to save him from the life she lived and the people she attracted.

Escher listened to his mother's revelations and wondered how he could have got things so wrong. His brain was fogged with confusion and whatever drug she'd given him, he needed to sit and process what she'd said and maybe in time he could formulate some questions. They found a bench which overlooked the East River and sat staring in silence at the green-grey water. The morning sun fully announced its arrival and lit the sky to a brilliant cerulean blue. A lone cloud meandered its way across the sky, before gently floating off into the distance taking with it all the wrong that had happened between mother and son.

It was 5.50 am, in a few hours excited children would arrive for a ride on Jane's carousel. It was time for Escher and Mariam to leave. A bloodied man and a hollow faced, drug bleached woman would be conspicuous in such a place. Soon after would come the tourists, perusing their guidebooks and reading about how, where and by whom the horses were carved.

Back at the car Escher started up the engine, the sun warmed interior of the vehicle began to lift the chill from his extremities, but in his heart, there remained an iciness the kind of deep cold even a furnace could not dispel. A thought came to him, a thought of retribution, of how after all these years, those who perpetrated crimes upon a small child and his drug addicted mother, could be found and punished.

'We gotta go back.'

'Go back? What you mean Babba?'

Escher pulled out of the parking space and turned onto Main Street.

'We gotta get her.'

'Get who?'

'Lucy.'

'Lucy who, why?'

'We need the mirror, so we gotta get her.'

'Mirror, what mirror?'

Escher turned on to Plymouth Street toward Brooklyn bridge.

'I can't explain, it's something you gotta see.'

He turned right onto Anchorage place and looked at his watch. He needed to get across the city to the site where he'd buried Lucy's still breathing body, he hoped to God the workmen were late starters. If Lucy was dead already, he'd never find the ones who'd done those things to him and his mom.

He grabbed Mariam's hand and squeezed it.

'Don't worry Momma, I'm gonna make everything ok.'

Roxanne Dinsdale

Printed in Great Britain
by Amazon